HARD
CHARGER

MEGHAN MARCH

UNAPOLOGETICALLY SEXY ROMANCE

ABOUT HARD CHARGER

Lia has known true darkness—and not just because of the power grid failure nine months ago. She has faced evil and emerged a survivor. Now if she could just make the two men she wants see her as whole and not broken ... maybe she'd have a chance at the future she's determined to claim.

Cam and Travis have been brothers-in-arms since their days as Force Recon Marines, and there's nothing Cam wouldn't do for his best friend—except let him have the woman Cam's been patiently waiting for. But when Lia shocks him by saying she wants them both, he has the decision of a lifetime to make. Lose the girl, or lose his best friend.

In a world where nothing is certain, can three people find their way to love?

*Warning: This book includes two sexy as hell Marines, one strong woman determined to have them both, and a whole lot of sex—the dirty kind. Proceed at your own risk.

Hard Charger is a novella set in the *Flash Bang* world.

Flash Bang is available on all major retailers.

CHAPTER 1

Darkness.

The world knew darkness the day the lights went out, but Lia didn't know the true meaning of the word until three days later. That was when those who preyed on the weak had stolen the life she'd known. And since that time, Lia was the first to admit she was weak.

"You're gonna be okay. What's your name, sweetheart?" The voice penetrated the haze that had settled over Lia like a protective blanket. She didn't want to break through the barrier that protected her from reality. Then she'd have to *feel*. She wanted to stay numb.

"You with me, sweetheart? You're going to be okay. We're the good guys."

The good guys. The words floated through her brain. *Are there any of those left?*

Lia didn't believe him, but she didn't have time to focus on that. He kept asking for her name, disrupting her self-imposed exile from reality. As awareness filtered through, so did the ache that throbbed all the way down to her bones. With every word, the pain intensified. Her face throbbed, and her scalp felt like it'd been torn off in chunks.

"What's your name?"

"Lia," she murmured, just to get him to shut up and leave her alone.

He didn't ask again ... at least not before the blessed darkness claimed her once more.

Lia surfaced against her will, but every time, she dragged herself back into the darkness; however, not before realizing she was no longer chained. She no longer smelled as her own filth. Crisp, white cotton sheets were tucked up around her body. She didn't know who'd done it, but the white hurt her eyes after spending so much time in the dark.

The door opened, and a man stepped inside the dimly lit room. Lia slammed her eyes shut, not wanting him to know she was awake. Not that pretending to be asleep had saved her before; only banishing her consciousness to that tiny corner of her mind had offered protection from them.

"I know you're awake, sweetheart. I can tell by your breathing."

Lia froze.

His voice was quiet, but the rumble reminded Lia of a thunderhead rolling in across the lake with a summer storm.

"No one's going to hurt you. I know it's going to take a long time before you believe that, but it's true."

She couldn't stop the huff of disbelief that shifted her chest. *Shit. He'll know for sure I'm awake.* Lia's eyes snapped open, wanting awareness for the first time since her world was destroyed beyond recognition. She told herself it was because she wanted to see this new threat, but part of it was *that voice.* How could a voice that deep and masculine carry the promise of safety?

It couldn't.

Lia shook off the crazy thoughts and bared her teeth. *Yes, I've become an animal. Come at me, motherfucker, and I will tear you to shreds. Or at least go down swinging.*

He didn't smile. Didn't laugh at her impossibly ridiculous display of courage. He came closer—but slowly.

"You're gonna be okay. No need to get all worked up. I'm just here to check on you and see how you're doing."

That goddamn voice. It wrapped around her, and the comfort was even warmer and stronger than what the darkness had offered. He was the light.

"You saved me," she breathed.

A short nod. "We got you out of there."

Lia shook her head. "No. *You saved me.* You took me away from them."

Another short nod. "You weren't up to walking out under your own steam. We just helped you out. Sure you'd do the same."

A showdown with crazy inbred rednecks who were armed better than the Michigan Militia for some bedraggled stranger? Ummm ... not likely.

Then again, Lia wasn't built like this guy either. She catalogued his every trait: six-four if he was an inch, with a chest so dang wide it threatened to split the seams of his T-shirt. He didn't look like a body-builder though. He was solid muscle, but it seemed like the kind of muscle a man developed because he used his body as a tool. A weapon.

In that moment, Lia knew this man was dangerous. And judging by the fact he'd carried her out of her worst nightmare—he was more dangerous than the crazy inbred and well-armed rednecks.

"Who are you?"

"I believe I asked you the same question several times, and I only got a little slip of a name. You up for a trade?"

A trade. He asked. Didn't take. This was new and different in Lia's reset world—one resembling more of a horror movie than reality.

She could do this. There was nothing harmful in giving him her name anyway. "I'm Lia."

"You got a last name?" he asked.

"McLaren."

"Lia McLaren. It's a pleasure." The way his voice wrapped around the syllables again unleashed a tide of warmth within her. She could listen to him read the phone book and it would chase away the monsters ... even better than the darkness.

"I'm Cam." He stepped forward and offered his hand, and Lia couldn't control her instinctive flinch. He froze.

Only weeks ago—or maybe only days—Lia had never known the jaw-cracking pain of a man's closed fist connecting with her face. But that was before she found the darkness. Once she did, she never felt anything again. God only knew what other horrors she would've witnessed. Still, she couldn't control the urge to shrink away as he advanced.

"I'm not gonna hurt you, sweetheart. Just want to shake your hand and wrap up these introductions properly."

He held his hand out to her, but there was so much more than his hand hanging in the air between them. A shining thought bloomed in Lia's mind. This hand was an opportunity. An anchor. A chance at safety again. It was irrational—crazy, even—but that's what she saw when she looked at it.

Did she dare?

Lia closed her eyes for a beat, and the darkness called her back to its sweet oblivion. She snapped them open. *Enough darkness.*

She pulled her hand out from beneath the sheet and reached out until her palm slid against his. She expected to want to yank it back immediately, but the urge never came.

His voice was amazing.

His touch was better.

He was the light.

She'd had enough darkness.

She curled her fingers around his and clung.

CHAPTER 2

Cam stood outside the clinic and stared at the camp, trying to erase the haunting images from his brain—the woman he'd just left inside, but covered in mud and filth, chained to a pipe like an animal; the way she'd laid limp in his arms as he'd carried her mile after mile through the woods; and the bruises that still covered nearly every inch of her exposed skin. There was still no guarantee she'd pull through, but he liked to think she was a fighter, a hard charger—much like Rowan Callahan, the woman who had alerted them to her existence and the reason the rescue mission had been launched. Rowan was a feisty brunette who was keeping two of his former Force Recon teammates, Graham and Zach, on their toes because of her relentless determination to get home to her family. She was too reckless and stubborn to realize that even though she'd made it this far, the world outside the walls of Castle Creek Whitetail Ranch was nothing like it had been only seven days earlier. Although, Ro should've been aware considering the trek she'd made all the way from Chicago. Her journey—which was her own crazy-ass story—had been fairly uneventful until she'd heard a woman screaming and followed the sound to a camp of rednecks in the woods. That screaming woman had been Lia. Ro had almost ended up their next victim, but her sprint away from danger had sent her right into the fence line of the ranch. Cam shuddered to think what would've happened to Lia if Ro hadn't demanded they save the pitiful woman she'd seen dragged on her knees through the dirt.

Firebombing the camp hadn't been enough. He wanted every single one of them dead—but they'd only gotten two of them.

And the fact that they could firebomb a camp just showed how much the world had changed in the last week—because seven days earlier, he and the entire crew of former Jar Heads had been running a successful and exclusive deer hunting operation in rural Michigan. Six days ago, the entire world had gone dark in what they were assuming was a complete power grid failure. Due to Graham's foresight and their general mistrust of the government after seeing *way* the fuck too much over the last decade of their military careers, Castle Creek Whitetail Ranch was also probably the most intense doomsday prepper compound in the entire state. They'd left nothing to chance. From impeccable defenses to stores of food, weapons, supplies, alternative sources of power and beyond—they had everything needed to carry on in the face of a complete collapse of modern society. If the TV show *Doomsday Preppers* had ever heard of them, they would've put the rest of those wannabes to shame.

Given that operational security was the first step of successful prepping, no one knew what they were hiding in the bunkers beneath these buildings. The walled compound was surrounded by hundreds of fenced acres and some of the finest whitetail that could be hunted in the Midwest. If the grid had gone down even a few days later, they would've had a camp full of early season hunters, but as it stood, the only residents of Castle Creek Whitetail Ranch were ten former Force Recon Marines, one wife, one five year old daughter, and now Rowan and Lia. They all thanked God that Jonah, the only married member of their crew, had had the brilliant luck of falling in love with, and marrying, a former Mennonite. Part of the reason they were set up to run so efficiently without a steady supply of electricity was Allison's unique upbringing. So if their solar, wind, or microhydro power systems ever died, they'd still be fine, albeit a little less comfortable. As it stood, they were ready to ride out the apocalypse in *style*.

"How's she doing?" Travis asked.

Cam stared at his friend for a few moments before answering, "Only time will tell."

CHAPTER 3

After eight months, Cam hadn't made his move.

"Thanks for walking me back," she said, standing at the door of the cabin she shared with Erica Callahan. Erica was Rowan's spitfire of a sister who'd come to live at the ranch shortly after Ro.

"You don't have to thank me every night, Lia," Cam replied.

"You don't have to walk me every night either, but you do."

He studied her face, and she knew what he was thinking: *I do have to, because you still jump if most any man in this place catches you off guard in the dark.*

Even after all these months, she still dropped her eyes when confronted with the direct gaze of the giant, alpha males inhabiting the compound. But, to her credit, she'd come a long way in that time. She might jump, but at least she was no longer looking for potential weapons and cataloging all available exits every time she entered a building.

That was something, at least.

And besides, not *all* of the men set her on edge in a negative way. No, there were two who set her on edge in the most frustrating, but delicious way possible.

And there was the problem.

She shouldn't want them both.

Her thoughts were interrupted by Rowan's voice carrying across the camp.

"You don't need to carry me everywhere, Conan."

Lia and Cam both looked toward the mess hall that sat about fifty yards away—their previous destination—and the glow of the solar light that revealed Graham holding a very pregnant Rowan in his arms. One problem with living in a compound was that privacy was the scarcest of resources.

The door to the big, low building opened again, and Zach stepped outside. Lia knew she should look away, but she couldn't.

"You know arguing isn't going to help at all, don't you?" he asked her.

"I'm pregnant, not an invalid."

"Hush, woman. This baby is coming any day now. Don't expect me to let you do a damn thing," Graham replied.

The reason she couldn't look away? That. And that was also why Lia couldn't get the idea of two men out of her mind. Because she saw it every day.

Their protectiveness. Their care. Graham and Zach's absolute devotion to Rowan.

Lia wanted that.

She just wasn't gutsy enough like Ro to go after it.

For months she'd waited for Cam to make a move, but he continued to handle her with kid gloves, as if every time he touched her he was waiting for her to flinch like she had the first time he'd come toward her.

What did she have to do to show him she was ready?

If she couldn't even figure that out, how the heck was she going to figure out how to ask for *both* of them?

"You sure you don't want to climb one of the watch stations, drink, and watch for shooting stars instead of heading to bed?" Travis asked.

The invitation came out of the dark from behind her ... and from the man responsible for the other half of her confusion. He'd been absent at dinner because he was on watch duty. Lia only knew this because she had both Cam and Travis's watch schedules committed to memory. She'd also been expecting him to knock on her door—like he did most nights—to make sure she was all settled in and to find some way to make her laugh.

Cam's head swung around, and his hand settled on Lia's lower back. The heat from his palm burned through her shirt, and she wondered if the gesture was instinctive ... or possessive.

A girl could only hope.

"No way in hell is she climbing a damn tree, drinking, and then falling out," Cam shot back.

Travis lifted his chin, and his eyes left trails of shivers down her body as he surveyed her.

"I'd never let her fall. You know that, don't you, babe?"

The words hit her with a surge of warmth. Combined with the heat flaring off Cam, she was surrounded.

The feeling faded when the awkward silence rose up between them. *Oh yeah, they're waiting for me to answer.*

"I—I ... of course I know that." Lia cleared her throat and fumbled for the door handle. "But ... I'm ... tired. So I'm ... going to bed." She yanked open the door and ducked inside. As soon as it slammed shut behind her, she sagged against the wood.

"What are you running from now, girl?" Erica asked.

Lia jerked at the voice of her cabin mate.

"Sorry," she hurriedly apologized. "I didn't know you were in here. I wouldn't have slammed the door."

Erica was reclined on her bed, a rechargeable light hooked to the top of her book. She raised her eyebrows. "Considering I'm reading *The Art of War* for the zillionth time, I'm not too bothered by the interruption. How did these guys not think that romance novels deserved a place in the bunkers? What do I have to do to get some good old fashioned smut in here?"

She tossed the book on the bed and leaned over to turn up the wick on the oil lamp. A soft yellow glow filled the room.

"So what gives, chica?"

Lia pushed off the door and kicked off her shoes before crossing to her bed and plopping down in the middle.

"Nothing."

"Lie."

Lia cut her eyes to Erica. "It's not a lie. There's absolutely nothing up right now. I have no idea what you're talking about."

The other girl's eyes narrowed. "Oh, honey, it's going to take years before you can bullshit the bullshitter. I'm a master, and you, grasshopper, are a novice."

"Maybe you should lay off the Sun Tzu ... your metaphors are getting ... weird."

"And maybe you should cut the crap and just tell me what's bugging you." She held up a hand. "Unless you want me to tell you what I think it is."

Oh God.

Lia froze. If Erica knew...

"No—not necessary—"

But Erica had already crossed her arms. "So here's the deal as seen by yours truly."

She paused for what had to be effect, and it was working. Lia's nerves were climbing the charts.

"You want to bang Cam, but you're not sure how to go from the friend zone into the fuck zone."

Well, that was accurate—but not all of it. Lia bit her lip and said nothing. She didn't know what to say exactly.

"Come on, you gotta give me something. I'm right, aren't I?"

Lia knew if she didn't tell Erica something, she'd never let go of it.

"Well ... yeah."

Erica's assessing gaze pierced her. "But that's not all."

"Oh my God, what are you? Some kind of psychic?"

"No. I'm just perceptive. But ... I'm not entirely sure what the rest of your problem is here. With a few well-placed hints, Cam would for sure make a move. That guy is probably jacking off constantly thinking about you. He's all protective, and it's adorable. He wants you, there's no doubt about that. He's just worried that you're—"

Erica's words cut off abruptly, and Lia knew why.

"He's worried I'm too messed up to handle it."

For the first time since she'd entered the cabin, Erica looked uncomfortable. "Well ... you did go through some messed up shit, baby girl. Any guy who's not a complete dick is going to tread lightly around that."

"It's been *months*. I'm not—"

"Still jumping at shadows or the other guys? I hate to break it to you, but you are."

Lia glared at her. "Has anyone ever told you that you don't have to say *everything* that comes into your head?"

Erica shrugged. "I consider my lack of filter a gift. But seriously, if you want Cam, you've got to show him you're ready for more."

Lia knew she was right. She needed to just come out and show him unequivocally that she could handle it. But ... it was the second piece of the equation, or really the *third*, that she didn't know how to address.

Erica picked at her nails, and Lia dredged up the courage to ask for advice.

"What if I wanted Cam ... and someone else?"

Erica's eyebrows hit her hairline. "Whoa ... didn't see that coming." She pressed her palms together and tapped them against her lips. "Are you saying you can't choose ...

or are you talking about what my big sis has going on? Two hulking beasts of men devoted to seeing to her every comfort and orgasm? Because I'm seriously hoping it's the second..."

Lia swallowed down the urge to claw back the words. In for a penny... "I want what Ro has," she blurted. "I ... how can I not want that? They'd both die to protect her, and I've never seen three people so happy."

"Or bicker so much and make up so loudly," Erica added. "But I know what you mean. It's tempting as hell." Erica dropped her eyes and picked at the quilt below her. "You're not the only one with some serious envy over that situation."

This time it was Lia who was shocked. "You're ... that's what you want too?"

Erica shrugged and looked up. "We're not talking about me. We're talking about how to get you back on the horse, so to speak. So, here's what you're going to do..."

CHAPTER 4

Cam crossed the compound and headed for the command post. The last thing he wanted to do tonight was sit in his cabin and stew on things he couldn't change.

Zach was seated at the desk, checking in on the hour with the guys on watch. In the months since the world had gone to shit, they hadn't decreased their vigilance one bit. As remote as they were, and away from any major cities, they'd been virtually isolated from the chaos in the outside world, but that wasn't to say they hadn't had to fight to defend their territory. They had, and they would do it again and again. It gutted him to think of the people they hadn't been able to help, but that was the first rule of OpSec—keep your mouth shut about what kind of supplies you had, or you'd have nothing left. Curiosity seekers were swiftly encouraged to move along or eat a bullet. It was harsh, but it was necessary. They had women and a child on the ranch to protect, and trying to help the world would mean that none of them would survive. Brutal reality.

When spring had rolled around, they'd heard rumors that the country's population had been decimated. Starvation, disease, lack of medical care. Those who had survived were the strongest and most resilient. On recon missions, he'd been surprised and downright fucking pleased to see that several of the farms and towns in the vicinity had found ways to survive and even thrive. Crops were already springing up—and not just theirs. It was a whole new world out there, and it would take amazing determination and flexibility to keep it going. The other rumors were more troubling. The government was finally getting its shit together and trying to figure out how to rebuild society. That society sounded a fuck of a lot like a fiefdom of old. They'd heard stories of people being rounded up and taken to work camps and centralized farms—against their will—but on the pretense of being saved. Fucking ironic how the government hadn't stepped in until after the population had already been culled of the sick and the weak. It certainly hadn't been an accident.

"You gonna just stand there and stare at the wall or did you come to talk about something?" Zach asked.

Cam jerked his gaze to Zach. "Just thinking about shit."

Zach leaned back in his chair. "You and me both. Now that the weather is getting nice, we're getting more curious people checking out the fence line. As much as I want to help, there's no fucking way I'm putting Ro at risk by bringing some jackass inside the walls."

Cam nodded in response. It was a dilemma they all struggled with. It had been beaten into them in the Corps that you never left a man behind, and it was their job to protect those who couldn't protect themselves. Like they had with Lia. But trying to protect them all would mean protection for none.

Lia. Fuck. What was he going to do about her? He wasn't sure how much longer he could hold back. He'd never wanted a woman more, but he'd also never been so fucking scared that he'd scar her for life if he told her what he wanted from her. Because he wanted everything. Mind, body, and soul.

She had no clue that he already considered her his. He'd made it fucking clear to every man within these walls that she was off limits. And only his best friend seemed to miss the memo.

There was no better person to ask for advice than the man sitting in front of him.

"Before you and Graham worked out shit with Ro, were you ever jealous of him being with her? Worried that he would take her from you, and you'd lose your shot?"

Zach laced his fingers behind his head and leaned back in his chair so it balanced on two legs.

Of course, Zach being Zach, he didn't just answer the question, he cut to the heart of the matter. "You worried someone is going to snake Lia from you before you man up and make your move? Which, by the way, has taken way too fucking long in my opinion."

Dropping into the chair situated at the radio counter, Cam rubbed a hand over his face and into his hair. It was getting shaggy again, and it needed a cut. But the torture of sitting through Lia washing it—massaging his head and neck in a way that made it impossible for his dick not to get hard—and then having her fuss over him with shears and clippers was more than he could handle right now. He was barely hanging on to his sanity where that woman was concerned. To have her so close and still not be able to touch her, to take her, was going to wreck him.

"What the fuck am I supposed to do? You didn't see her that night—chained to a wall like a dog. They fucking *broke her*, man. How could she ever trust another guy to touch her?"

"I don't think you're giving her enough credit. She's come a hell of a long way since then."

"She still jumps every time one of you comes near her." *All but one*, he added to himself. And that fact burned.

"But she doesn't flinch when you touch her. I agree that it's a situation you gotta handle as carefully as a live IED, but man, I think you're fucking up by not going for it."

The door swung open, and exactly the person Cam didn't want to see stepped inside.

Fuck. The man was as close as a brother. He shouldn't feel that way.

"What's happening? Any excitement tonight?"

"Not a fucking thing," Zach replied. "Unless you count Cam having his panties in a bunch over—"

Cam's death stare shut Zach up mid-sentence.

Travis's gaze swung to Cam, the challenge and interest easy to read. His attention slid back to Zach. "Cam's got his panties in a bunch a whole hell of a lot lately."

"Don't fucking talk about me like I'm not here."

"Then stop being a bitch where Lia's concerned. You haven't made a move. Staked your claim and did nothing to follow through. You either want her or you don't, and I'm sick of fucking waiting for you to make up your mind."

"So you've decided to poach? That's a real standup move of you, man."

"It's not poaching if you're never gonna make a move."

Anger burned hot and fast through Cam.

"She's not the kind of woman you can just *make a move* on. And if you weren't so fucking self-absorbed, you'd see that."

Travis lifted his chin. "You got anything else you want to say to me? Because I've had about enough of your shit." His fists flexed, and his stance turned defensive. "In fact, I think it's about time we settled this once and for all. We take this shit outside, and the last man standing gets to make his move."

Zach grinned, and Cam wanted to punch the look off his face. "This may be a whole new barbaric fucking world, but we're not at the point where you fight for a woman."

"Doesn't mean she has to pick me," Travis said. "Just means that you back off and let me take my shot."

"She won't—"

"I think you need to stop making judgments for Lia and let her make her own. She's a grown woman, and she's stronger than you think."

The words hit Cam in the chest, and the truth of them curled around him. Apparently it was time—time to nut up or shut up. But first he had to end this bullshit with Travis. They were brothers in arms, and the wedge that was being driven between them over Lia was poisoning that brotherhood.

"Fine. But you gotta know there's no way in fuck I'm giving her up."

Travis's smile was wily and knowing. "Then you better be prepared for a hell of a fight. Because there's no way I'm losing my chance with her."

"When?"

"Now works for me."

"Whoa, boys. I think we need to take a step back and evaluate what the hell you're talking about here," Zack interrupted. "And we also need to make sure we maximize the entertainment value of what I'm sure is going to be a kick ass spectacle. So, let's do it up tomorrow." He nodded at Cam. "Give you a day to think about what you've got to lose."

Cam shoved out of the chair and headed for the door, stopping six inches in front of Travis. "Fine, but once this is done—however it ends—you and I are burying the hatchet and getting back to normal. I'm sick of this shit."

Travis nodded. "I'd expect nothing less. No sore losers."

Cam held his hand out, and Travis grasped his arm and thumped him on the back. "We'll be good, brother. No matter what."

CHAPTER 5

In the mess hall, Ro was glowing, and Lia once again inwardly sighed with envy. She'd always wanted her own kids, but it seemed like that was never going to happen.

Ro started to stand, but Zach laid a hand on her shoulder and kept her in her seat. "I got your plate, babe. You stay. You want blueberry pie? Allison's getting low on filling, so if you want it ... now's the time."

Her smile was brilliant. "Do you even need to ask?"

Zach dropped a kiss on her lips and grabbed her plate. Then he turned to Lia. "You want some, too?"

Lia fought the urge to drop her eyes from Zach's. Today was a new day, and today she was reclaiming a piece of herself that she'd lost when she'd been dragged off to hell.

Instead of giving him a jerky nod or shake of her head, she stared him straight in the eye. "I'd love a piece, thank you."

Zach's eyebrows rose, and a smile curved his mouth. "You got it."

When he turned to head for the kitchen, Ro's attention landed on Lia.

"So ... you know why there's no one here for dinner, right?"

Lia had noticed the mess hall was strangely empty. Only Allison and her daughter were there along with Zach and Ro. "Are the guys having a meeting or something?"

Ro's eyes lit with something that Lia couldn't quite identify.

"Not exactly..."

A shiver of concern worked through Lia. "Then what?"

"They've decided to go old school barbarian and settle a dispute with their fists."

"What?" Lia demanded. "Who? And what for?" None of that made any sense.

"Cam and Travis. And *you* are the what for."

Zach came back carrying two plates with giant slices of blueberry pie.

Lia completely forgot that she was supposed to be afraid of him. "What do you know about this? Where are they fighting? *Why* are they fighting?"

Zach set the plates on the table. "You should probably just eat your pie, and pretend this little troublemaker didn't say a damn word." He looked hard at Ro. "You said you'd stay out of it, Ro. And just because you're pregnant doesn't mean I won't find a creative way to make you pay for not keeping your word."

"She deserves to know. This affects her more than anyone else." Ro's chin jutted playfully. "And maybe I want you to make me pay..."

"Jesus, babe. You're determined to get us to—" Zach cut off his words with a shake of his head. "I'll deal with you later." He looked to Lia. "You need to stay put. There's nothing to be gained by seeing this."

Lia shoved her chair back from the table, ignoring the mouthwatering aroma of the pie. "I'm not letting this happen. *No one* is fighting over me." A sick feeling settled in the pit of Lia's stomach at the thought of Cam and Travis fighting ... over her. Everything she wanted—the fantasy she'd constructed in her mind—crumbled to dust at the realization that they didn't want it too. *This is not how things are supposed to go.*

Ro reached out and snagged her hand and squeezed. "Don't freak out yet. If this is what it takes to get Cam off his ass and make a move, then it's a good thing."

Lia ignored her words. "Where are they?"

Zach slid his hand over Ro's mouth as she opened it. "You've meddled enough, babe. Leave it be."

"Fine. I'll find them myself." Lia spun and headed for the door. She made it two steps before she turned and grabbed the plate and took three huge bites of the pie. It was the last of Allison's canned stash; it made no sense to let it go to waste.

Once she was in the main area of the compound, she spotted Erica rushing toward the wall. She slowed to a halt at the sight of Lia.

"You coming or what?"

Lia didn't need an explanation. "Oh, I'm freaking coming."

Travis circled the man he considered to be his closest friend. But the last several months had put a shit load of distance between them. Wanting the girl your best buddy had staked his claim on threw a wrench in the easy friendship they'd always had. He'd still take a bullet for Cam, but he wasn't willing to let him keep sitting on the fence when it came to Lia. Travis had watched her slowly come out of her shell, and it had been so damn good to watch. Yeah, she still jumped around the other guys, but the way she was around him and Cam was completely different. Cam just needed a shove to get his head out of his ass. Regardless of the outcome of this fight, Travis wasn't giving up his shot at Lia. No ... he had a different plan in mind.

As Graham laid out the rules of the match, Travis smiled. Graham and Zach had shown him that their crazy arrangement could work. And Cam was his best friend ... so why the fuck not? He'd seen the way Lia looked at them both ... and the way she'd looked with longing at Ro, Graham, and Zach. He was willing to bet it all she wouldn't be the difficult one to convince in this situation. No, that honor would undoubtedly go to Cam, the possessive motherfucker.

They bumped knuckles, and Travis had to laugh at the fact that Jamie had had two pairs of MMA gloves in his sea bag. He also looked fucking jealous that he wasn't standing in the middle of their makeshift ring out in the field beyond the walls but within their fence line. Apparently they needed to add fight night to the list of entertainment activities. The guys on watch were expecting radio updates, so Jamie took the roll of commentator.

"You ready?" Graham looked from Travis to Cam.

Travis nodded. "Fuck yeah, I'm ready."

"Ready to get your ass beat," Cam growled.

They bumped gloves and stepped back.

Graham signaled for them to start and backed out of the ring.

Travis bounced on his feet, and they began to circle each other. He didn't waste any time charging Cam, right fist swinging out with a haymaker. Might as well set the pace early.

Cam dodged and threw a low jab that caught Travis in the gut. But he barely felt it with his pumping adrenaline.

"That all you got?" he taunted.

"Fuck you, man." Cam's fist flashed, and Travis was still laughing when it landed on his jaw. His head snapped sideways, and he caught a glimpse of brown hair running toward them.

"Fuck," he grunted.

"What the hell do you think you're doing? Stop!" Lia yelled.

"Oh shit," Cam said. He swung around and caught Lia in his arms as she stormed into the circle.

Travis's fists clenched in his gloves. He wanted to be the one to hold her. Fuck, he wanted them *both* to hold her.

He moved in next to them and pushed the hair that had slipped from her ponytail behind her ear.

Cam's eyes shot to Travis's, but instead of being pissed, he looked upset.

"It's okay, sweetheart. We're stopping, don't worry," Cam said, trying to calm her.

Lia shoved away from them both.

"Don't worry? *Don't freaking worry?* Are you serious?" She slammed a hand on each of their chests and looked from Travis to Cam and back again. "I don't know what you think you're proving here, but consider it over."

Travis's lips tugged with a smile. He felt like the last hazy filter that had clung to Lia had been ripped away. She was standing there, thrumming with life—and seemingly oblivious to the guys standing around them. Travis couldn't help but stoke her emotions higher.

"Calm down, baby. No harm, no foul."

Travis could've sworn that every man in the circle— and the sole woman—groaned. But he'd broken the cardinal rule—never tell a woman to calm down when she was pissed—on purpose. He'd lit the fuse with intent to watch her burn as brightly as she could.

"*Calm down?*" Lia's attention swung to him, and her hand dropped off Cam's chest. "You two are acting like I'm something you can fight over and *win*, and you want me to *calm down?*"

Cam laid a hand on Lia's shoulder and squeezed. "Let's take this somewhere less public." Travis was only partly surprised when Cam's eyes met his and held. "All three of us."

"Fine," Lia said, spinning and heading back to the wall. "I don't want the rest of the guys to hear what I have to say to you, so we can definitely do this in private." Her words were tossed over her shoulder as she stalked away, worn jeans clinging to her lusciously rounded ass.

Travis was still grinning at the feisty side of Lia that had come out full force when Cam punched him in the shoulder. "What the fuck are you smiling about? You just lost."

Travis shook his head. "Fuck no, brother. We both just won."

Cam frowned. "What the hell does that mean?"

"You'll find out. Just ... promise me you'll keep an open mind. Come on. Let's not make her wait."

CHAPTER 6

Lia seethed over the ridiculousness of what she'd just seen. They were so damn adolescent. Boys fighting over her like she was some kind of prize. Lia stomped back to the corrugated metal wall and pushed open the heavy porthole-style door. Footsteps crunched behind her. Good. At least they followed directions.

She went straight to her cabin and stood by the door. Erica was still outside the wall, and knowing what she knew, she'd keep her distance from their cabin.

Cam and Travis walked side-by-side, heading in her direction. She studied both men—Cam with his dark brown hair, curling over his ears. In another life, she'd been a hair stylist, but those days were long gone. Now, she looked forward to the times when Cam and Travis let her cut their hair. Allison handled all the others. Travis's coppery brown hair was now short, so Lia buzzed it almost every other week to keep it the length he liked it. He could've gone three, but Lia was pretty sure that his more frequent-than-necessary haircuts were because he liked how she massaged his head and neck. It was one small service she could offer in exchange for the roof over her head and the food in her belly.

They closed in on the cabin, and Lia stepped back, holding the door open.

"You sure you want to do this here?" Cam asked, looking uncomfortable as he stepped inside the obviously feminine space.

"My turf seems about right since you two decided I was worth starting a fight over."

"Lia—" he started, but broke off.

"What? No explanation?" She looked from one to the other. "One of you is going to tell me what the hell you were thinking."

Travis stepped closer and cupped her cheek. His possessive gesture—in front of the man he'd just been willing to go toe-to-toe with over her—sent shivers coasting down her spine.

Her eyes darted to Cam, and his frown made it abundantly clear that he didn't like the move at all.

"What makes you think you're not worth fighting for? Because I'm here to tell you that you're worth more than a fight. You're worth everything."

His words slid through her and settled somewhere in the melted puddle that used to be her heart. He lowered his hand, but the heat of his palm on her cheek remained.

"What was the point of all that?" she asked quietly.

"Lia, we need to talk," Cam said.

She raised her hand to stop him. "I ... I think it's my turn to talk." Grabbing all the courage she possessed with both metaphorical hands, she plowed forward. "I'm not broken. I mean, maybe I am, but I don't want you to think of me that way anymore."

Both men straightened.

"You may not be broken, but you're still fragile." This came from Cam, and Lia didn't like it. She might have been beaten and used by the men who'd taken her, but she refused to let it define her. That would be letting the darkness win.

"I'm not fragile. I'm ... goddamn resilient."

"We know you are, baby. You don't have anything to prove," Travis said.

"But I do. Because I'm never going to get what I want without proving that I can handle it." Embarrassment rushed over her at what they'd think if she kept going, and her cheeks burned. Dropping onto the bed, she covered her face with both hands as the sudden burst of courage deserted her completely. "Never mind. Just ... never mind. You should both go." So much for proving she could handle a damn thing.

The mattress sank on her right, and a hand touched her knee. Lia lifted her eyes to find Travis beside her and Cam crouched in front of her. Every nerve ending in her body surged with awareness of having them both so close at the same time.

Screw it. No one ever got anywhere by being a scared little girl.

Her thoughts were enough to give her whiplash, but Lia gathered strength from their proximity.

"I want you," she blurted.

Both men froze. For a few moments, no one in the room seemed to even *breathe*.

Cam commandeered one of her hands and squeezed. "Which one of us?" he asked quietly.

Travis laced his fingers through hers and pulled their twined hands onto his lap.

Lia wished she could have *both* hands back so she could hide behind them again, but that would just be adopting the scared little girl mentality again. She forced herself to meet Cam's eyes, terrified of what she'd see in them when she admitted what she wanted.

Two deep breaths steeled her courage, and then she replied, "Both of you."

Again, silence descended over the cabin, but each man squeezed her hand, giving her the faintest ray of hope. There were no accusations, no outbursts. Just ... silence.

Until Travis cleared his throat and spoke. "Can't say I'm disappointed to hear that, if you mean what I think you mean."

Cam's eyes left hers and jumped to Travis. "What the hell are you talking about, man?"

Lia watched Cam's face rather than Travis's—but it was Travis's words that gave her hope.

"You're my best friend, and I can't believe you think I'd try to snake the girl you're hung up on, man. I wasn't fighting you to steal her, but to make you admit you wanted her. Because I want her, too. And I think we've all seen that a triad relationship can work just fine."

Lia's mouth dropped open. He'd stolen her words. But she didn't care, because this meant at least one of the two men was thinking exactly the same way she was.

Cam released her hand and bolted to his feet.

"What the fuck are you talking about? You think she wants..." His stare pinned Lia. "Is that what you're saying? Or are you just saying you don't know who to choose?"

Lia sank her teeth into her lower lip while she gathered that courage from moments ago. "I'm saying I don't want to choose, and ... for the first time in a long time, I'm saying I want it all. Both of you. Together."

Unease churned in her stomach as she waited for his response. A dozen emotions flashed across the rugged planes of his face. Oh hell. This wasn't going to be good at all.

When he'd finally finished processing, his mouth set in a flat line. "This is really what you want?"

Lia held her breath before saying, "Yes."

Cam nodded. "I need to go. I have watch tonight. I need some time to think, so I know what the hell to say."

Her heart sank to her stomach ... until he did something he'd never done before: he leaned down and brushed his mouth over hers in a swift kiss.

"Don't freak out, sweetheart. I'll be back." The words were whispered against her lips, and then he left.

"That went better than I expected," Travis laughed.

Lia turned to him, their hands still tangled. "You ... you want that too? For the three of us to be...?"

Travis shrugged. "Why not? It obviously works with Graham, Zach, and Ro ... and I can't lie and say I don't think it'd be hot as fuck to have you between—" His words cut off before he said the last.

Heat flashed through Lia at the same thought she'd had over and over.

"Fuck, I swore I wouldn't push you or say anything to make you uncomfortable, and I'm already screwing it up. I should go too. Whatever is decided, we need to make the decision together." He lifted her hand to his mouth and pressed his lips to the back of it. "We'll talk tomorrow and figure this out."

Lia nodded dumbly as he turned to leave. Her thoughts had already started to retrace what just happened when Travis paused, hand fisted on the wood of the door.

"Fuck it. I can't leave without kissing you."

He turned, crossed the small room in a single step, and dropped to his knees in front of her. Lifting his hand to cradle her jaw, Travis said, "Tell me if you have a problem with this."

"Uhhh ... no problem," Lia stuttered.

"Thank God, because I've been thinking about tasting you for so damn long, I can't wait any longer."

A small sound escaped from Lia before Travis tilted his head and his mouth found hers—a slow, sweeping brush of lips, then the gentle tug on her bottom lip with his teeth.

"Open for me, baby. I want to taste you." Travis breathed the words, and Lia obeyed—because in this moment, she couldn't think of anything more right than tasting him too.

Lia parted her lips, and Travis's tongue swept inside. Within moments, all her senses were flooded with him. His taste—smooth and masculine. His touch—confident yet comfortable. His scent—clean man and the outdoors. She gripped his shoulder with one hand, leaning into the kiss, wanting more of it—more of *him*.

Travis's hand slid into her hair, and he kissed her deeper, giving her exactly what she craved. Lia was losing herself in the sensations—eyes closed, heart hammering—when Travis abruptly pulled back.

Not ready for this to be over, Lia tried to draw him back, but his soft smile stopped her.

"I've gotta stop now while I can still make myself leave."

"Oh," Lia said quietly, blinking up at him.

"But Christ, you're sweet. We'll figure this out soon, because there's no other alternative. I'm not sure how much longer I can go without kissing you again."

Her lips formed into a small O, and Lia watched him leave, heat and the need for *more* coiling in her belly.

Well. That had been unexpected.

CHAPTER 7

Cam strode to his watch post, head full of the crazy shit that Lia and Travis had both spouted. Share? What in the ever-loving *fuck*?

Lia was his. Sure, he might not have made his move, but that was because she was ... fragile. It wasn't like they didn't have time to take things slow. Almost nothing was for sure in this new reality, but one thing was absolutely fucking certain: he would never let anything happen to her, and he would never give her up.

Her words echoed: *I'm saying I want it all. Both of you. Together.*

Before today, he would've sworn that there was nothing he wouldn't give her. But ... he didn't know if he could give her this.

He was early for watch, and Graham was still in the perch when he began to climb the ladder.

"You in a hurry to sit in a fuckin' tree?" he called out.

"Shit. Sorry. I'll let you get down first."

Graham hefted his M-16, and made his way out of the tree. He dropped the last few feet to the ground, landing in front of Cam.

"Forget how to tell time?" Graham asked.

"Nah. Just ... needed something to do."

"I take it Lia didn't like the fight idea?"

"Not exactly."

"She chew you out?"

Cam looked at the ground. "And then some."

"I've known you a long time, man. So what the fuck is eating at you?"

Shit. Graham might seem like a stone wall, rather than a human being, most of the time, but as the former leader of a Force Recon team, he knew how to read people. If there was anyone who could give him a legit opinion on what Lia and Travis were saying they wanted, it would be Graham. He lived it. He and Zach had been sharing women since long before they'd claimed Ro. They'd already had their dynamic down, and ... other than one drunken night on leave, he'd never had a three-way.

Hell, he'd forgotten about that night. It had been him and Travis. They'd shared a sexy blonde they'd met at a bar. She'd refused to choose who she wanted to go home with, and Travis had offered up the solution of not making a choice.

Cam had been just drunk enough to think it was a fucking fantastic plan. But that was some random bar hookup. This was *Lia* they were talking about. The woman he'd been working on getting close to for months. The woman he was already half in love with because of her quiet strength and her unwillingness to let the darkness win.

Fuck it. He might as well just spill, because every minute he didn't, they were both derelict in their duty by not having the watch post manned.

"After she finished telling us what assholes we were for fighting over her, Lia said ... she didn't want to choose. She wanted us both."

Graham lifted his chin. "She wants you both ... together?"

Cam nodded.

"So?"

"So?" Cam sputtered. "I've never had a three-way relationship. I don't know how to do that shit. I've never been any fucking good at sharing. And sharing *her*? I ... I don't think I can do it, man."

Graham scrubbed a hand over his face. "Look, I'm not the one you should be asking for relationship-type advice. That's Zach's area. He's the one who's into talking about his *feelings*. But I will say this: If your choice is to share her or lose her, which do you choose?"

"When you put it like that..." Cam didn't like the options Graham had laid out.

"And if your choice is between having her and making sure she's getting everything she needs or leaving her unsatisfied, which do you pick?"

"So you're saying that even if Travis backs down gracefully—which that fucker has yet to do in his life—that part of her is always going to be unsatisfied with what I can give her by myself?"

Graham shrugged. "Hard to say, but is it a risk you're willing to take?"

"But how the fuck do I *share* her without wanting to rip his hands off every time he touches her?"

"Do you want to rip his hands off every time he touches her? Because if you do, you're gonna want to rip his dick off even more."

Cam opened his mouth to say *hell fucking yes*, but Graham held up a hand. "Think about it before you give me some knee jerk answer. You and Trav are like brothers, and he's crazy hung up on Lia too. You cool with taking that away from both of them just because you're being pushed out of your comfort zone? You're a fucking Marine. Man up, assess the situation, and make a decision you'll be able to live with. No one's telling you what's right or wrong, but you've also got the luxury of not living in a society that's going to judge you for your choice. Everyone's too busy trying to fucking stay alive for that shit." Graham slapped him on the shoulder. "Now get up in the tree and stay sharp."

With Graham's advice sinking in, Cam climbed up to his post and stayed sharp. It was going to be a long fucking night.

"Do you mind measuring out the ingredients for those biscuits?" Allison asked.

"I'm happy to help. That's why I'm here," Lia replied, putting an overly cheery note in her voice. *Please put me to work so I can stop thinking about how badly I've screwed everything up*, she silently added.

"Everything's already set out; I just need to run Little Miss here out to the facilities."

"I'll have them rolled out before you make it back," she promised.

The door to the kitchen closed behind Allison, and Lia watched for a moment as she walked her adorable little girl across the compound toward their cottage, before turning back to survey the kitchen. Allison had already started the big, black wood-fired oven. Once again Lia thought how lucky they were to be in one of the few places where life seemed somewhat normal. Having power and running water was a luxury that few others could claim. And being mentored by a woman who had taught her to bake from scratch, garden, can fruits and vegetables, help manage the aquaponic garden that provided fish and veggies year around, and develop myriad other apocalypse-savvy skills? Priceless.

With every little thing she'd learned, she'd clawed back a shred of confidence, and those shreds began to weave together and give her the strength to finally ask for what she wanted.

So much for not thinking about things ... because once again her mind went to Cam and Travis and their reactions to her declaration. The brush of Cam's lips over hers ... and Travis's drugging kiss. At least she knew they both wanted her; it just remained to be seen what Cam would decide. The waiting and wondering was the worst part.

Lia pushed aside the worries and measured the ingredients left on the counter in the quantities written on the recipe card in Allison's neat handwriting. She was rolling out the dough when the kitchen door swooshed open again.

"I'm almost done. These should be ready to go in the oven in a few minutes."

"Good, then you have time to talk when you're finished."

Lia stilled at the deep, rumbling voice. It sure as hell wasn't Allison.

She didn't look over her shoulder at Cam. She wouldn't. Because if she looked, he'd see her laid bare.

She wanted this—*them*—so badly she couldn't hide it any longer. And now that they'd both had their lips on hers? The longing for what could be cut through her on a visceral level. Her carefully constructed defenses were more than down; they lay crumbled at her feet.

"You want to talk?" she asked, dumbly repeating what Cam had just said.

His booted feet thudded on the wide-planked wood floor of the mess hall kitchen until the heat from his body radiated against her back. His palms landed on the counter on either side of her.

"Yeah, sweetheart. We have a hell of a lot to talk about." The words, and the breath that carried them, fluttered the hairs next to her ear.

Lia's nipples puckered against the tank top she wore—no bra, because women's undergarments were one of the few items the men of Castle Creek had failed to have the foresight to stock. But she was lucky enough that she didn't really need to wear one. Though, the man standing over her shoulder could easily tell the effect he was having on her body.

"I was afraid you said everything you had to say yesterday," Lia replied, the words coming out more like a question than a statement. But at least her voice didn't shake, so that was something.

"Sweetheart, that was just the beginning of the conversation. There's a lot more to talk about. So you finish up with what you're doing, and we'll be waiting."

He made it sound so simple. Like they would just talk it out, and yesterday hadn't been completely humiliating for her... *Wait, did he say* we'll *be waiting*?

Cam stepped back, and Lia found the courage to glance over her shoulder at him. His black T-shirt stretched across his wide chest. "We?"

His eyes dropped to her chest for a beat before coming back up to her face. *Well, no need to ask if he'd noticed the high beams.* "I'll round up Travis. Seems like we need all three of us if we're going to discuss this."

Lia wrung her flour-covered hands in front of her body. "Where?"

His answer was the equivalent to a dare: "Our turf this time. Can you handle that?"

She schooled her expression to give nothing away, including how many times she'd thought about what could happen behind the closed doors of the cabin Cam and Travis shared. She swallowed hard. "Fine with me."

A chin jerk, and he was gone.

CHAPTER 8

Admitting that he had no fucking clue what he was doing wasn't Cam's strong suit. He'd always prided himself on being prepared with multiple contingency plans if shit went sideways. But this ... this, he didn't even have a Plan A to go with, let alone his normal backups.

Share the woman you were hung up on with your buddy because she wanted you both. No, he didn't know what the fuck to do about that—but he absolutely wasn't walking away.

Still, the fact that *this* was what Lia wanted stunned him. Fuck stunned, it *amazed* him. She'd been through hell, regardless of what she actually remembered, and the fact that she wanted any man, let alone *two* men, was a testament to her strength and resilience. *Is this what it would take to make her feel safe and secure?*

Uncrossing his arms, he paced the cabin, only stopping when the screen door creaked open. Cam swung around, expecting to see—hoping to see—Lia at the door. But it was Travis.

He shoved down the disappointment, because actually, this was for the best. They needed to work shit out between them first, and they hadn't had the opportunity to do it.

"So, you got a plan here?" Cam asked, re-crossing his arms over his chest and studying his best friend. He dropped his arms to the side, almost as soon as he crossed them. He needed to get his head out of his ass and a defensive posture wasn't helping.

Travis cocked an eyebrow. "You're always the one with the plan. Thought you'd have this one worked out already."

Cam huffed out a laugh ... or at least he was shooting for a laugh, but it came out sounding a lot more like a grunt. "No plan this time. Flying blind here."

"A conversation this important, and you've got nothing? That isn't like you."

Travis's easy acceptance floored him.

"What do you expect me to say? Yeah, it's totally cool that the woman I've been falling for since I carried her out of hell doesn't just want me, but she also wants my best friend."

Travis studied him. "We need to be on the same page before she gets here, so I suggest you tell me right now which way you're gonna go."

It was now or never. Nut up or shut up.

Cam squared his shoulders and met his best friend's gaze. "I'm in. I've got no clue how this is gonna go down, and if it all falls apart, I'll damn sure be the one picking up the pieces. But if this is what Lia wants, there's no way in fuck I'm gonna tell her 'no' if you're on board too."

Travis held out his hand, elbow crooked, palm up. Cam stepped forward and clasped it.

"Okay then," Travis replied. "And if shit falls apart, we deal with it. Together."

"Agreed. As long as she comes first in every decision we make, I don't think we can fuck this up too bad."

"Friends no matter what?" Travis asked.

"No matter what," Cam repeated. They released each other and Cam settled onto the couch to wait. Travis dropped into his favorite recliner. They didn't have to wait long.

Lia slowly crossed the compound toward Travis and Cam's cabin, eyes alert—like someone might come running out of the shadows with a chainsaw. The creepy thought pulled her back to the rundown camp of the men who'd taken her prisoner three days after the world had gone dark. She'd lived alone, in a little rental cottage at the end of a wooded road. She'd been so proud of her place, because she'd worked her ass off to save enough to get one on a lake. Cosmetology hadn't proven to be a crazy lucrative career, but she'd made enough to keep herself happy and moving out of the apartment on a busy main road had been a victory. She'd loved the serenity of the lake, even if the house had been tiny. But that serenity had proven to be her undoing. Three days had taken her through all of the water in her house, and she'd been so damn thirsty that she'd ventured down to the lake, desperate for a drink. It had been a horrible mistake—for two reasons.

First, because she hadn't been the only one who had known about the lake. Two men in dirty flannel shirts and patched jeans had been a hundred yards from the bank where she'd drank directly from the lake and then filled her bucket. When they'd seen her, they'd started to move in closer. When she'd run, it'd been like firing a starting pistol, because they'd chased her to her front door and broken it down. Her brother had been coming up the drive, walking back from sourcing supplies. He'd gone head-to-head with the rednecks, but unarmed against two men with guns, he'd had no chance. The last thing she remembered was her brother's dead body, blood pooling from three bullet wounds—the side of his head, his chest, and his shoulder—before she'd dropped to her knees and everything had gone black.

She'd woken up later, throwing up over and over again. For two days she'd heaved until there was nothing left. The best she could figure was bacteria from the lake. She'd been so weak, and the men had been so pissed that she was sick that instead of helping her recover they'd...

Lia shook off the thought as the darkness threatened to creep in. *No*, she wouldn't let the darkness win. She wouldn't think of them. They were dead. Like her brother. Her stomach twisted, and her eyes burned. She'd been so helpless and weak, but no longer. Now she was strong enough to ask for what she wanted. She was ready to quit existing and *live*.

She squared her shoulders and approached the door.

Can I really do this? Yes. I can and I will. Because she only got one life, and even if it was this crazy *end of the world as you know it* life, she was going to make the most of it. And making the most of it meant taking what she needed and experiencing something amazing. There had been no guarantees before, and there *certainly* weren't any now. So this was Lia McLaren taking life by the balls.

She grabbed the door handle and pushed it open, not bothering to knock. She'd never been in this cabin before, but she was determined to start this crazy thing like she meant to move forward. No more timid Lia—only bold, strong, confident Lia. The girl she had been before, and was determined to be again.

She stepped inside, and the two gorgeous men looked at her. Cam with his dark, curling locks and dark eyes, and Travis with his green eyes and short coppery-brown hair. One serious and brooding, and the other lighthearted and fun. Both incredibly handsome and protective and all of the things she could want in a man. Was it any wonder she wanted them both and couldn't bear to choose?

Both men rose from their seated position, thoroughly filling the small front room of the cabin with their presence. Both men were big, but Travis was the shorter of the two. Probably about six-two, but his shoulders were every bit as wide as Cam's. They were both striking. Their work around the compound had kept their bodies in top physical shape.

Equally panty-meltingly gorgeous.

Except in this instance, Lia had opted to skip the panties. Sexy lingerie was non-existent these days ... and her ragged cotton ones hadn't exactly inspired naughty thoughts.

And that action in itself was a declaration: That she wasn't just coming here to talk. No, she was coming here for action.

"Thank you for coming," Cam said.

"Of course."

"You want a seat?" Travis asked, gesturing to the couch that Cam had been sitting on.

"I'm good to stand," she replied.

A warm hand landed softly on her shoulder. "Sit, sweetheart. We've got some major stuff to discuss, so you might as well get comfortable."

Lia swallowed, her throat drying up like the Sahara. "Umm ... okay." *Major stuff to discuss* meant that Cam wasn't shutting this down immediately. It meant ... she might actually be getting her wish.

Holy freaking shit.

Lia sank into the comfortable, old couch and laid her hands palm-down on her thighs.

At least she lay one of them down, because Cam also sat, reached out, and laced his fingers through the other hand and pulled it between them.

Lia's eyes went to his, her brows rising.

"First thing you gotta know, sweetheart, is this is all about you. Nothing goes forward unless you're on board completely. I know some ideas seem good until you start putting them into practice, so you gotta know that any time you want to call this off, you can."

The hope and excitement that had been building within Lia fell. "So ... you're already expecting this to fail? Or for me to bail?"

"*No*," Travis interrupted. "We're putting it out there that this only happens if you're totally comfortable. There's no point in beating around the bush—you've been through hell, and we both know that you're taking a heck of a leap asking for what you want. Have no doubt that we want to give it to you, but we also want you to know that just because we start this, it doesn't mean you're locked in. You can say 'no' anytime you want."

So they were giving her a free pass if she wanted an out. With the panic attacks she'd had every time she'd gotten physically near a man those first few months, that might have been necessary, but not now. Still, this seemed to be important to them to establish, so she would leave it alone.

"Okay. Duly noted. What's next?" She pointed to her shirt. "You want me to strip?"

Cam squeezed her captive hand. "Slow down, sweetheart. We're in no hurry. We've got all the time we need to ease into this."

And that's the problem, Lia thought. She'd been easing into this for months, and had just now finally worked up the courage to ask for what she wanted. If she didn't make the move, there was no telling how long her courage would last. She refused to let this opportunity pass her by simply because the thread of courage slipped from her fingers.

"I don't want to take this slow. I've been taking things slow since I got here. I'm ready."

"What if I'm not?" This came from Cam—the man who was always sure of himself and ready for anything.

It hadn't occurred to her that her readiness didn't have any bearing on theirs. Was she forcing them into this? *Omigod. What if the only reason they're considering it is out of pity?* She thought about Travis's words. *You've been through hell.* Were they just doing their civic duty by giving the poor, damaged girl what she needed to get herself whole again?

Oh. Hell. No.

Shit. And here was the problem with making the first move. She'd never know if they would've ever made one or if she was the only one really feeling this. It wasn't like there were many other available women within the walls. What if they were just agreeing because she was the only viable option?

Doubts assailed Lia from every angle.

This is a horrible idea.

She stood, bolting from the couch, but her hand was caught fast by the still-seated man.

He tugged her back.

"Lia, what the hell?"

"I ... this was a mistake ... I'm ... I shouldn't have done this. I'm sorry. I shouldn't have—"

Travis was off his seat and in front of her within seconds.

"Calm down, baby. Let's just chill. If you're having second thoughts, we can talk about it."

"No, not second thoughts. Fifth, sixth, and seventh thoughts. Hell, maybe hundredth thoughts. I didn't know what I was thinking. That you'd actually be interested. That you'd actually want me. I should never have presumed—"

The grip on her hand tugged her closer, and within moments she was seated on Cam's lap, his arm curling around her waist to anchor her in place.

"What are you doing?" she demanded. "You said I could go whenever I want. I want—"

"You told us what you wanted, and now you're getting something in your head that shouldn't be there. You're not leaving until we get at least a few things straight—and the first one is, *we both want you more than you could ever imagine*." Cam whispered the last words directly into her ear, and the heat of his hand pulsed against her belly.

Travis dropped onto the couch beside Cam and squeezed her other hand. "The one thing that's absolutely not in doubt in this room is how much we want you."

"Oh," the word came out on a breath. "Okay." Well that was one less thing Lia needed to freak out about. Everything else still loomed large. Like what happened if they went for it and it didn't work out. Now that she was between them, all the things that could go wrong—and cost her both of them—crashed down.

She struggled to stand, and Cam finally released her and she stumbled to her feet. Travis's hand on her arm steadied her.

"I—I ... maybe I was wrong. Maybe I can't do this." *God, what a mess.*

"Talk to us, baby," Travis said. "Tell us what's going through that beautiful head of yours."

"I can't lose you both," she blurted.

She couldn't find the courage to look at Cam, so she focused on Travis.

"You're not going to lose us," he protested. "No matter what happens, at the end of the day, you will always be able to count on both of us."

"But our friendships? And the two of you—your friendship? What about that? You can't tell me that if this goes south, I'm not responsible for destroying all of that."

Cam stood, and his body pressed against Lia's side.

"You can't tell me you haven't thought about this six different ways to Sunday. You've weighed it all."

He was right; she had thought about every contingency, but she'd also somehow whitewashed all of the risks that were involved with sparkles and glittery rainbows. Because that's what you did with dreams that were far off in the distance: You played up the benefits and played down the sharp edges. She was about to tell them that she needed more time to think, when Travis beat her to it.

"How about we just hang out tonight—as friends? We play some cards, have a drink, keep it low key. We've never really hung out with an eye toward something more. Let's find our rhythm and see what makes sense for us."

"Cards?" Lia repeated.

Travis nodded and pulled out the drawer in the coffee table, producing a deck.

Cards. She could do cards. Low key. Low stress. Low freak out. She could do this.

They were being hustled. That was Travis's only thought as he shucked off his pants and tossed them to the floor.

"Cheers," Lia laughed, toasting him with her shot of whiskey before she sipped from it. She didn't toss it back and drink the whole thing. No, she savored it, because she'd said she didn't want to waste it.

Travis didn't care, though, because he didn't want Lia to get drunk. The way things were headed, he could see tonight getting a whole hell of a lot more interesting.

He caught another look that Lia darted between him and Cam. Both of them were stripped down to nothing but their boxers. Socks were gone too. Lia, in contrast, had only removed her necklace and a single sock.

The woman was a fucking card shark, and goddamn if Travis didn't find that hot as hell. He shook his head.

"How'd you learn to play cards like a Vegas poker legend?" Travis asked.

Lia shrugged, looking completely at ease on the cushion next to Cam. Which was fucking phenomenal. He wanted her chilled out and comfortable with them—and the fact that she wasn't freaking when the clothes started to come off was a good sign indeed.

"My dad played when I was a kid. He taught my brother and me. I went to poker night once a week at my brother's place until..." her words trailed off and her expression darkened. "You know. Until the shit went down."

Both Travis and Cam's attention landed on the same thing. "You have a brother? How the hell didn't we know that?" Cam demanded.

This time, Lia grabbed the shot and tipped it back, swallowing until the glass was empty. She set it on the table with a *crack*.

"Because he's dead."

"When?" Travis asked softly. He leaned over the coffee table, grabbed her hand, and squeezed. He needed the closeness when it was obvious she wasn't into talking.

Cam's hand landed on her knee in a similar gesture of support. Even though Travis knew whatever she was going to say next was going to suck donkey balls, he was happy that the three of them were already pulling together like a unit.

"The day they took me," Lia bit out. "Those assholes killed him. Three rounds and he was down."

"Then I'm even more glad we fucking ended them and lit up their camp like the Fourth of fucking July," Cam said, wrapping his arm around Lia's shoulders. He pressed a kiss to her temple. "I'm so sorry, sweetheart. I had no idea."

She squeezed Travis's hand. "Wish I'd known sooner, would've made them suffer even more."

Lia smiled sadly. "He died protecting me. Hell of a big brother, right?"

"The best," Travis replied.

Lia dropped Travis's hand and reached for the bottle. "I think that deserves another drink."

Neither man protested as she filled her shot glass again and tossed the whiskey back.

The card game all but forgotten, Travis focused on Lia. How incredibly fucking amazing she was. She'd been through so much, and she'd clawed her way back every single time.

Travis folded his cards onto the table. "Think I'm done with this hand."

Lia set her glass down on the table more carefully this time. "I think I'm done with this game." Her eyes landed on Travis before shifting to Cam. And then she did something completely unexpected—she grabbed the hem of her T-shirt and pulled it up and over her head.

The black cotton floated to the ground, and Travis damn near swallowed his tongue at what Lia unveiled: No bra—just ripe, delicious tits. Bigger than a handful and tipped with perfect, brownish-pink nipples.

Instinctively, Travis reached for the shirt she'd just discarded and started to hand it back.

"What are you doing, sweetheart?" Cam asked, his words steady and calm. Travis had to wonder if Cam's heart was hammering as hard as his at the sight of Lia's perfection. Lia turned, her tits bouncing, and Travis swallowed back a groan at the movement.

Fuck. This woman would destroy him. No doubt about that.

"I'm done playing games. You say you're in, then let's make this happen. I don't want to think about anything tonight. I want to push all the other bullshit aside, and just *feel*."

Travis fisted the shirt in his grip. Were they really ready to jump in headfirst? Whatever happened here tonight would change everything. He'd been the one to push this—even more than Lia had—so if it fell to shit, it was largely on him.

Cam must have been operating on the same wavelength—no surprise there since they could practically finish each other's sentences—and asked, "Are you absolutely sure? Because we can all put our clothes back on and finish our card game and call it a night."

Lia shook her head. "I'm done playing. I want real."

Cam looked to Travis, and Travis only hesitated for the briefest of nanoseconds before he nodded.

"Okay, then we're still gonna take it slow. Get used to each other. And you're gonna let us call the shots from here on out, but if we do anything you don't like, or anything makes you uncomfortable, all you have to say is *stop*. In here, no means no and stop will bring it all to a halt."

Lia nodded, her fingers digging into the cushion of the couch. "Okay."

"Then I think Travis should come over here and give those gorgeous tits some attention while I finally get a taste of those sweet lips of yours."

Travis didn't have to be asked twice; he stood, gripped the coffee table with both hands, and lifted it out of the way. Lia's eyes widened as he dropped to his knees in front of her.

"Can't have anything getting in my way."

Her mouth opened into a small O, and that's when Cam leaned in, cupping her jaw, and turned her face to his. Travis waited for the jealousy, for the surge of possessiveness that even he wasn't sure he'd be able to hold back ... but nothing came. He was too caught up in watching Lia's eyelids sink closed and the sweet little sounds coming from her lips. He couldn't wait to make her moan so loud the entire ranch could hear it.

Cam pulled away. "Just as sweet as I imagined." He brushed her hair out of her face and pulled it back behind her shoulders.

Travis stayed motionless until Cam looked to him and raised a brow. Travis shook out of his momentary paralysis and tilted Lia's chin back down to him.

When her eyes met his, he skimmed the backs of his fingers along her jaw. *Hell.* Her skin was so goddamned smooth. He followed the arch of her neck down to the hollow of her throat and slowed at the swell of her breast.

"So fucking smooth." He continued his descent, skimming the backs of two fingers over her puckered nipple.

Lia released a quiet moan and her nipple hardened further. He trailed back up to her chin, then back down the slope of her other breast, circling the areola.

"Can't wait to have these in my mouth." He smiled at Lia's absent nod. Watching her every reaction, he rose up on his knees, ghosted his lips over hers, before following the same path he'd taken with his fingers.

CHAPTER 9

Lia arched forward, pushing her chest toward Travis's face. Every nerve ending flared as the hint of his lips whispered over her skin. Her mouth opened on a quiet moan and her head dropped back as his lips closed over her nipple.

"Omigod," she breathed.

Cam's big hand once again cupped her jaw and turned her toward him, and his mouth lowered over hers.

His lips—so firm and smooth—touched and teased before his tongue joined in and demanded entry.

As soon as she acquiesced to the demand, he buried his other hand in her hair and devoured.

She would forever associate Cam's unique flavor with the mildest bite of whiskey. Her tongue dueled with his, and she leaned into him, moaning as Travis cupped one breast and kneaded while his tongue flicked and circled her nipple.

The sensations coming from both parts of her body were overwhelming. So long without any sensual contact with a man, and now she was overloading—from just a kiss and a man playing with her breasts.

The overload didn't scare her. No, it made her want to fan the flame—take it higher, hotter, further. She wanted more. More touch, more taste, more sensation. She wanted it all.

Lia threw herself into the kiss and pushed her chest out into Travis's touch. Her hands shot out, one burying in Cam's hair and the other gripping Travis's shoulder.

Travis must have thought her touch meant to stop, because he lifted his head.

She pulled back from Cam's mouth. "Don't stop. Why are you stopping?"

Her eyes flicked open and swung to Travis.

"You don't want me to stop?" he asked.

Breathlessly, she replied, "No. Don't stop."

Travis looked to Cam. "Want to move this to your bedroom?"

His words brought no fear—just a rush of molten heat between her legs. Without waiting for Cam's response, Lia pushed herself to her feet and took a step in the direction of the bedrooms.

A calloused hand wrapped around her wrist.

"Hold on, sweetheart." Cam's voice held a note that she couldn't identify. There was desire, but also ... caution.

Lia tossed a glance over her shoulder. "I don't want to hold on, unless it's to both of you."

Cam pulled her back, and then turned her to face them. "We're not having sex tonight."

"Wait, what? Why not?" Lia sputtered.

"Because we're not jumping into this a million miles an hour. We're going to take it slow. We're in no hurry, and we're going to savor this. Savor *you*."

"But what if I want—"

Cam's expression darkened. "I told you we would call the shots. Consider this us doing that."

"But—"

Travis reached out and squeezed her other hand with his. "But nothing. We've waited this long, one more night isn't going to kill any of us." The corners of his mouth curled into a smile as he glanced to Cam and then back to

Lia. "But that doesn't mean we aren't going to tease you until you come harder than you've ever come in your life."

Heat burned Lia's cheeks, but it was a punch of lust, not embarrassment, that was driving it. As of right now, she'd made the decision to check her inhibitions and shyness at the door.

"Okay."

Both men rose, and between them, Lia felt sheltered and tiny. At 5'6", she wasn't used to feeling *small*—at least not in the normal world, but here at the ranch, all of the men seemed to be giant, so feeling short wasn't a new development. But when two had men flanked her before, her instincts would riot, sending panic racing through her. But right now—between these two men? She felt nothing but content. She loved that they were big and strong and able to protect her.

Cam slid his fingers through hers, and Travis gripped her other hand. Together, they walked toward the bedroom, with Cam leading the way. Crossing the threshold, her eyes landed on the king-sized bed, covered in a navy blue quilt, taking up the majority of the room.

They all paused at the foot of the bed.

"Second thoughts?" Cam asked.

"None," she replied, courage rising even stronger.

"You're fucking amazing, Lia. You need to know that. Fucking amazing."

She looked up at them both. "Thank you. You make me feel amazing."

"You want me to make you feel even more amazing?" Travis asked, sinking to his knees in front of her. "Because I want my mouth on this sweet pussy, too. I've been dying to know how you taste for so goddamn long."

Turn down oral? Not likely. Lia nodded absently. "Yes. Yes to more amazing."

Travis's fingers found the button of her jeans and the zipper before peeling the denim down her legs.

"Whoa, sweetheart, you forget something here?" Once again, Travis ran the backs of his knuckles over skin.

Confused, Lia looked down and then laughed self-consciously. "Ummm ... I didn't think my panties were the sexiest ... so I kind of left them off."

Travis leaned in, and she felt his next words spoken against her navel. "No need to wear them ever again as far as I'm concerned," he breathed. He dragged his lips from her belly button all the way down to her pussy.

She shivered at the contact, anticipating the first brush of his tongue against her most sensitive flesh.

Big hands landed on her hips, and her eyes flew to Cam's. He said nothing, just slid behind her until he was seated on the bed and lifted her easily into his lap. He hooked one leg over each of his and ran his palms up her belly to cup her breasts before dragging his thumbs back and forth over her nipples.

Lia melted into him, dropping her head back onto his shoulder. Fuck. He was solid heat against her back. Any other thoughts flew from her head as they seemingly coordinated their movements.

Cam's forefingers and thumbs pinched and rolled her nipples as Travis spread her lips and dragged his tongue up her slit.

"Oh my God," Lia moaned. Pleasure unfurled as they continued. Travis, sucking and licking and tasting, and Cam, tugging and teasing. Travis's lips closed around her clit as desire sparked through her.

She'd wondered if she'd be able to come, and hadn't been convinced of the fact, but the orgasm was already building. She rocked her hips forward, encouraging Travis—wrapping a hand around the back of his head and scraping her nails down the back of his buzzed hair—something she knew he loved.

He groaned against her pussy, and Lia's own moan broke free.

"That's it, sweetheart. Let us hear how much you like it." Cam's words rumbled in her ear, zinging straight to her nipples.

The shivers gathered low in her belly as Travis teased her entrance.

She'd never survive. No way. The shivers gained substance until Travis slipped a finger inside her and Cam pinched down on her nipples—then she shook as the first orgasm she'd had in nearly a year washed over her. It wasn't the slamming-into-a-brick-wall kind of orgasm; it was a delicious swell of pleasure.

She pushed Travis's head away when the swipes of his tongue became too much for her to handle.

He pulled back. "Didn't think you could look more beautiful, but that look on your face is proving me wrong. Gonna have to put that look on your face as often as goddamn possible."

One second she was sitting up, and the next she was bent back over Cam's arm. Her hands flew up, gripping his chest, but the easy smile on his face quieted her panic.

"I had to see it for myself," was all he said.

These men ... wow.

It was her turn. Lia tried to scramble off Cam's lap, but he held her fast.

"Where do you think you're going?"

"I want to—"

"Let us make you come again," he interrupted.

And then she was flat on her back with Cam propped on one knee beside her.

Well ... okay then.

Cam woke in the middle of the night to a curvy body curled around his side and a small hand on his chest. Normally it was the nightmares that woke him, but this time it was the hair—wild dark hair—tickling his pecs.

His lips quirked into a contended smile.

His arm was asleep, and he didn't fucking care. He loved it. His gaze dropped to Lia's hip, where Travis's hand rested.

He waited for the rush of jealousy to come ... and kept waiting. Instead, he felt a breath of relief. If anything ever happened to him in this less-than-certain world, Lia would never be alone. Not just because of the clan they had at the ranch, but because Travis would be just as protective over her as he would be.

This relationship—as crazy as it seemed—might be the best idea they'd ever had.

Falling asleep with this woman in his arms, knowing that the man who'd watched his back through some of the most deadly scenarios imaginable was there to cover them both was unbelievably comforting—and Cam wasn't the kind of guy who usually sought comfort. He was used to charging ahead and hoping like hell enemy fire never found its mark. But this ... this felt right.

He closed his eyes and found sleep again.

CHAPTER 10

Lia's eyes flicked open, and the first sensation to hit her was heat. Waves and waves of it coming off the two huge, hard bodies bracketing her on the bed.

Oh shit. I fell asleep, she recalled. *After that amazing orgasm.*

All the stress of the day—combined with the whiskey—and she'd lost the battle against sleep after they'd taken turns unleashing torrents of pleasure within her. Cam had pressed a kiss to her hair and Travis a kiss to her cheek. They'd both said the same thing: *We're not rushing things. Just sleep.*

She'd let her lids fall closed and had tumbled into the most delicious dream. Except it wasn't a dream, even though it was still completely dark outside.

A big hand cupped her breast, idly stroking her nipple—which was now puckered and hard.

Another hand was ghosting fingers across the flat plane of her stomach. With each pass, the fingers moved south.

Lia lifted her head off the chest she was using as a pillow. Cam. He met her eyes.

"This okay?"

Heat cascaded through her as his hand moved even lower still, just north of her clit.

The thumb on her nipple increased its pressure, and Travis's voice came over her shoulder. "And this?"

"Yes. All of it."

This was what she'd been waiting for. What she'd been wanting. Two bodies, four hands, all focused on her. It had been a heady idea, and now it was an intoxicating reality.

She waited for the darkness to sneak up and demand she run from the sensations sweeping through her, but it never came. All that existed was the shimmer of pleasure and the swell of emotion for each of these men.

So she responded the only way she could. "More."

"Anything you want, sweetheart," Cam said, sliding his hand lower. "As long as you're sure."

"I'm sure. Soooo…" she trailed off when the word became more of a moan than anything else.

"I think she's sure, man."

Travis's thumb and forefinger worked her nipple as Cam's hand slid lower to cup her.

"Fuck, sweetheart, you're so wet. Already soaking my hand."

And she was. Hell, she'd never been so wet in her life.

He slid one finger between her pussy lips and skimmed her opening before dragging it up through her wetness to her clit.

She arched against Travis's hard chest, pressing her lower half into Cam's hands. She didn't bother to keep track of whose hands were where as the tendrils of lust began to wind around her body, turning her sounds to whimpers and outright begging.

"Omigod, right there."

"You talk to God a lot, baby," Travis whispered in her ear. "I'd rather hear you scream my name. Both our names."

Cam's thumb stayed on her clit, the exquisite pressure driving her hips harder into his hand, and his finger plunged inside her.

"She's going to be screaming both our names when we get inside her this morning."

Her eyes shot open at Cam's words, and she found his dark ones fixed on her.

"We're ... right now?"

Cam lowered his head and nipped at her lips before kissing her deeply.

"Unless you're having second thoughts, baby, this is happening. If you touched my cock right now, you'd know exactly how hard I am for you. Fucking dying to get inside you. We both are. I spent the night with this hot little body next to me, and damned if it didn't make it so much easier to sleep—and so much fucking harder. Having you so close and still not knowing is the best kind of torture."

Lia's heart hammered, and it wasn't just because of the orgasm that was building low in her belly already. It was because of what was going to happen here. Was she truly ready for this?

Travis's lips landed on her neck and his teeth scraped along the length of it. "A taste of you wasn't enough. We want it all. If you're sure that's what you want."

The upside of this happening right now meant that they'd stop asking her if it was what she wanted. Because she did. So much. It was time to go all in.

"Stop asking me, and just fuck me already," she said, and Cam took that exact moment to slide a second finger in and work some black magic with his touch, because her orgasm burst through her like sparks off a live wire.

Reaching out with one hand in front of her and the other behind, she grabbed both men as equal lifelines. "Oh God."

"Travis and Cam, baby," Travis chuckled darkly in her ear. "Not God."

But her head was already falling forward on to Cam's shoulder, and her nails dug in.

"Fucking Christ. Your pussy is so goddamn tight. I gotta get in there." Cam slid his fingers out.

"Then what are you waiting for?" she asked, her eyes opening once more. As soon as the words were out, she realized they were something the old Lia would have said. The Lia who was confident and sure of her own sexuality. The Lia who she'd thought had died in the darkness. Pride in how far she'd come rose within her, and any lingering qualms she may have had about what was going to happen dissipated.

Cam's smile caused another flood of warmth in her belly, and she rolled to her back. She wanted to see Travis too. She wanted to see them both. Her mind whirred with logistics.

"How do we? I mean ... it's been a long time since I've..." So stupid that she was shy all of a sudden. She was about to have one man in her pussy and one in her ass, and she was embarrassed to tell them this wasn't her first back door rodeo? That it'd just been a while?

Travis reached down and smoothed the hair back away from her face. "We take it one step at a time. You don't have to take us both, baby. That's like going from crawling to running an Olympic sprint."

Lia swallowed. "I've never done the ... three-way before, but I've had anal. I just remember needing to go slow to make sure ... you know..."

"That doesn't mean we need to rush this, baby. We've got all the time in the world to explore."

Lia's mouth closed into a pout, and Travis leaned down to cover her lips with his and swallowed any protest. When he finally drew back, he groaned.

"Fuck, I want this mouth."

Lia's eyes darted from one man to the other, and Cam reached over to the bedside table and pulled out a condom. The vast stores of them on this ranch were laughable, but that was what happened when you had ten men stocking the place.

"Can you handle that, sweetheart? Travis in your mouth and me filling up that tight pussy of yours?"

Lia's inner muscles clenched at the thought. She nodded, unable to find the words to describe how much she wanted that. It'd been so long. She was desperate for them both.

"Tell me yes, and we'll give you everything you can handle," Cam prompted.

"Yes." The word came out strong and sure. "I can handle anything with you two."

Travis watched as Cam lowered his head and traced his tongue along Lia's lips.

"She's so fucking perfect."

His hands found her tits again and cupped and squeezed, thumbing her nipples into hard points until Lia moaned into Cam's mouth. Travis couldn't wait to feel her moan on his cock. When Cam pulled away, Lia sat up and rolled to her knees and pressed one hand next to Travis's abs before tugging his boxer briefs down over his bobbing cock. He couldn't remember ever being this hard in his fucking life. He wasn't sure how long he'd last inside that sweet mouth, but he couldn't wait to find out.

Lia was eager, barely waiting for him to lift his ass so she could drag his briefs lower.

"You in a hurry, baby?" he asked, cradling her face with his hand. "Because we've got nothing but time here."

Lia's eyes flared, and she growled the cutest little growl. "If you think I haven't wondered what it'd be like to have your dick in my mouth, you'd be wrong. And I'm ready to stop wondering."

She turned her head to look at Cam. "And you. If you think I haven't thought about how good it'll feel to have you stretch me wide with your cock, you don't know me as well as you think you do."

Travis picked his jaw up off the floor. Who was this confident, sassy, *bold as ever-loving-fuck* woman? As soon as the question formed in his head, he knew he was seeing the Lia who'd existed before the shit had hit the fan. The Lia who'd almost certainly had men eating out of her hand and begging for more. The Lia he'd always hoped he'd get to see.

"You're fucking incredible, baby. No doubt about that."

He's right about that, Cam thought. Lia was more than fucking incredible; she was a goddamn goddess. And right now, she was waiting for her men to worship her. Naked, her tits hanging free, her ass out and perfectly rounded, he had to consciously slow his breathing or else he'd be rolling that condom on, sliding home, and coming within moments.

No, he needed to make this last. He needed to prove to her that they would take care of her every single fucking time, so she'd never question the decision they'd made. Hell, he needed to prove it to himself that this setup—the three of them—was better than it would be with just him and Lia by themselves. But seeing the way she looked at Travis, and the careful way he handled her, Cam had no regrets.

He tore the condom wrapper open with his teeth and dropped his eyes to position it and roll it down over his rock hard dick.

Lia swung a look over her shoulder at him, and it told him everything he needed as he lined up his cock with her entrance. Bringing a hand around her hip, he slid his fingers over her clit and lower to make sure her pussy was still dripping for him. She was soaked.

"Ready, sweetheart?"

It was happening.

"Yes, so ready." Lia replied with no hesitation before turning back to Travis and wrapping a hand around his length. "Are you?" she asked him.

"Fuck yes."

Cam pressed the blunt head of his cock against her entrance and pushed, stretching her wide.

She jacked Travis's cock as she moaned in pleasure at the invasion. It had been so long. And now ... with them...

Lia lowered her mouth to the crown of Travis's erection and swirled her tongue before sucking him between her lips. His hand cupped her jaw and lifted her eyes upward. "So fucking good. So fucking beautiful."

She took him deeper as hands skimmed down her sides and squeezed her hips. Then Cam began to thrust, and her groan vibrated along Travis's shaft.

"Oh fuck. Baby. Hell." Travis's fingers buried in her hair. She bobbed her head, slowly, as he helped control her depth and speed. She loved his guidance, the feel of being so full—Travis in her mouth and Cam in her pussy. How full would she feel once she had one of them in her ass and the other in her pussy? Cam's hand found her clit and played, and she bucked back against his cock while working Travis's. They fell into a perfect rhythm that she couldn't have choreographed better if she'd tried.

The swirls of orgasm were already solidifying, and she wondered how long she'd be able to hold out against it—or if she could drag them both over the edge with her.

She squeezed tight on Cam's cock and sucked Travis harder. She wanted them just as mindless with pleasure as she was becoming.

And then she felt slickness on her ass. Unable to turn her head to see what Cam was doing, she had to focus on the sensations—the press of a finger against the pucker of her ass.

There was no fear—no worry—just another deeper, darker shiver of pleasure coursing through her. She wanted whatever he wanted to give her because she knew he'd never hurt her, never take advantage. Lips pressed between her shoulder blades and the finger fought the tight ring of muscle before it breached her ass.

Another moan from her and Travis lifted her chin and fucked deeper into her mouth, his eyes on hers—passion and desire—and something even more than that—flaring in his brilliant green gaze.

These were her men.

Cam fucked her with his cock and his finger, and Lia's eyes slid shut as the threads holding her pleasure together snapped.

Travis pulled from her mouth, and she was too mindless to stop him.

"Baby, I'm gonna come," he growled. Her eyes snapped open, expecting to take him deep one more time, but instead he stroked his cock. "All over those gorgeous tits of yours."

Cam slammed home again and again until he groaned long and loud, and she had no words to offer them, only the sounds of her pleasure and a jerky nod.

As the hot ropes of semen landed on her chest, the heel of Cam's other hand pressed hard on her clit, and another orgasm followed the first.

Swamped with sensation, Lia's elbows collapsed, but Travis's quick hands caught and held her up.

For several moments, none of them moved.

And then finally, Cam slid out and they both rolled her to her back.

His eyes clouded with lust, he lowered his lips to hers and pressed the softest, sweetest kiss to them. Travis followed suit as soon as Cam moved.

Silently, they cleaned her up and covered her with a blanket.

Her eyes fluttered closed as they told her once more to sleep.

CHAPTER 11

Lia snuck into her cabin as the sun rose. Erica—who normally slept like the dead—shot wide awake.

"You're doing the Castle Creek Walk of Shame," she said, the words seeming so much louder in the previous silence of the cabin.

"Shhh ... Jesus. If I wanted the whole ranch to know, I'd just go sound off the alarm."

Erica smiled and rolled over onto her side, propping herself up on her elbow. "Sorry. I'm just ... I'm so excited for you!" She clapped both of her hands together—awkwardly, given her position. "So, tell me everything."

Sudden shyness filled Lia. She'd never been one to kiss and tell, but this was Erica, the girl who'd patiently helped coax her back into the world of the living.

"Ummm ... stuff happened."

Erica's eyes bored into her. "No shit. You just spent the night curled up between two hot-ass Marines, so of course *stuff happened*, sweetheart. I need more details than that."

The endearment—the one Cam had always used—sent her memory spinning to what had happened as the early morning sky had turned from black to gray.

She'd had sex with two guys.

Holy shit.

And then she'd freaked the fuck out because when she'd opened her eyes, reality had come crashing in. One question cycled through her brain on repeat: *If I lose either of them, will I lose myself to the darkness again?* They were her light, and she was terrified that by throwing herself into this headfirst, she might have screwed everything up. She was pretty sure she was in love with them—not because she'd slept with them, but because ... she'd finally let go of the tight grip she'd held on her emotions when she'd climbed into their bed—and now the fear slithered its way inside.

Even with her rioting thoughts, Erica's pout was actually quite endearing. "Why the hell are you back here already? Shouldn't you still be in bed doing *stuff*?"

Should she still be in bed? Well, probably. But part of the reason she'd left had been because she was trying to avoid *this* particular conversation.

She shrugged, deciding it wouldn't hurt to share a little. "They ... they were amazing. Patient, sexy, and it was ... mind-blowing." *So why aren't I still in bed?* she asked herself silently.

Erica lifted her hand to wipe a little imaginary drool off her lips. "Please, please, please tell me more. My sister keeps everything locked down tight, but you've got to tell me how it is. I mean, *two* sexy as hell guys?"

A smile tugged at the corners of Lia's mouth. "If you're so curious, why don't you try it yourself?"

Erica sighed. "You think I haven't tried? I swear, some of these guys are so damn stubborn they put even me to shame. That still doesn't explain why you're here instead of with them."

Lia considered for a moment before answering. "Because I'm terrified that taking this step was a huge mistake. What if it doesn't work? I could lose them both now."

Erica reached out and gripped Lia's hand before settling back on her bed. "Oh, hon. Don't lose faith. You're finally going after what you want. You've got to trust in yourself—and them. I know I'm just sitting on the sidelines, but that also gives me a little more of an objective view." She paused, pulling a pillow into her lap. "Those two watch every move you make. Not in a creepy way, but in a protective, possessive, *longing* way. They've been waiting for a sign from you, and you've just given them one in flashing neon lights. You're not the only one who put it all on the line here, and they stand to lose the ultimate prize—you—if it doesn't work out. With that kind of motivation, you better believe that they're going to do whatever it takes to smooth out any bumps in the road."

When Erica put it like that, a layer of the fear slid away.

"Thank you. For listening."

Erica flashed a brilliant smile. "Anytime, babe. Now, if you're not going to give me the dirty details, I'm going back to bed for a little while before I have to be up to help Allison with the laundry. Fucking hate laundry day."

Lia thought about stripping off her jeans and climbing into her own bed, but it didn't look nearly as inviting as the one she'd just left. Instead, she decided that she probably needed to hit the bathhouse for a shower.

Yes. A shower was a good plan.

Maybe then she could wash away the rest of her fears.

Lia leaned into the spray, letting the hot water beat down on her shoulders. Thank God once more for men who knew how to ensure a supply of hot water with alternative sources of power. Sliding a hand through her hair, she worked on rinsing Allison's homemade lavender conditioner away, enjoying a few more moments of heat before she turned off the tap and felt around for the towel she'd hung on the hook to the right of the showerhead. But her palm slapped tile instead of fabric.

"Looking for this?"

Her eyes snapped open at Cam's voice.

He held her towel clutched in his palm, just beyond the shower room. And he looked ... upset.

There was nothing to do but brazen it out. The shreds of the old Lia that had been knitting back together last night weaved a few more strands into place.

"Yes. Thank you."

Lia held out her hand for the towel.

"That's funny, because we were looking for something, too, this morning." Shock lit through her as Travis's voice—and form—joined the party and he stepped into her line of sight.

"Umm ... about that..."

Cam leveled his pained stare on her. "Did we push you too hard? Go too fast? Too far?"

"Did we hurt you? Scare you?"

Their words settled in Lia's gut like lead. They thought she'd bolted because of something *they'd* done.

"No. Not at all—"

"Then why'd you run, Lia?" Cam's deep voice sounded ... hurt ... as it wrapped around her name. "You had us fucking worried."

"I'm sorry, I just ... I needed to think."

If they'd looked upset before, now they both looked *troubled*—and that was putting it mildly.

"We shouldn't have—" Travis started.

"Fuck, I knew it," Cam said.

"Stop!"

Her voice echoed in the tiled shower room, and both sets of their eyes—one green and one brown—snapped to hers.

"It was just me, not you. I was freaking out because I think I'm..." Shit. She couldn't tell them this. They'd think she was crazy. They'd think she was ... just crazy. And clingy and God only knew what.

"You think you're what, baby?" Travis prompted, his eyes pleading for some kind of answer.

Cam flexed his hands into fists, and the veins in his arms bulged. His upset, his concern—every single emotion that was running through him seemed to be printed right on his face. They were both absolutely and completely transparent right now. Could she be anything less?

"I think I'm in love with you both."

The words hit Cam hard—like the punch of a bullet that had ripped through his shoulder, so near to his heart that they hadn't been sure he'd make it. But this hit? It threatened to drop him to his knees for a whole different reason—the reverberations vibrating through his body were pure and utter happiness.

"You're ... in love with us?" Travis parroted back to Lia.

Cam watched in awe as the woman he sure as fuck *knew* he was in love with nodded in response.

"Are you sure?"

She nodded again.

"Thank fuck," Cam breathed, crossing the space between them and wrapping her now-shivering form in the towel before dragging her into his body. "Because I know I'm in fucking love with you, sweetheart."

Travis moved in, his hands pulling back the mass of dripping hair from Lia's face. "Best goddamn thing I've heard since this whole fucking apocalypse dawned."

Cam released Lia from his hold only to allow her to be gathered up and crushed against Travis's chest. "I love you too, baby. So fucking much. Never thought I'd get my shot. Thought I'd be loving you from afar... watching you be with someone else. You letting us take this shot is ... so fucking amazing."

"So you're not changing your minds," she asked as she lifted her head and wiped the tears from her eyes.

"Why would we change our minds?" Cam asked, totally mystified.

"Because this is all so much, so fast. I mean ... like you said, from crawling to Olympic sprint. This isn't ... some normal progression of events."

Cam slid his hand down her arm until his fingers caught hers. He lifted her hand to his lips and kissed her knuckles.

"First, there isn't a single goddamn thing that's normal anymore these days. And second ... this isn't happening *that* fast. I've been hung up on you since the first moment you took my hand, Lia. This is where we've always been headed." He looked to Travis. "And the fact that I didn't count on this being a trio instead of a couple doesn't change a goddamn thing. Knowing that you have both of us to protect you and take care of you just eases my mind. It didn't take me long to figure out that there were more upsides to this than downsides. And seeing you take us both last night..." Cam groaned. "Never seen anything hotter."

Travis wrapped his arm around Lia's shoulders, leaned down, and kissed her. When he lifted his mouth, he added, "Whatever's going on in that beautiful head of yours—you gotta share. That's the only way this is going to work—a lot of communication."

She nodded. "Okay. I won't ... do the morning disappearing act again."

"You sure as hell won't," Cam agreed. "Because you're moving all of your shit into our cabin today.

Lia's eyes went wide.

Hell. Maybe he should've saved that little announcement?

"Wait, what?"

"It's not like we'd be able to hide this, even if we wanted to. And I don't know about you, but I don't want to hide jack shit."

Lia swallowed, then squared her shoulders and looked from him to Travis and back to him. "You're right. I just … I just hadn't thought that far yet. I guess … it makes sense."

"Damn straight it makes sense. We'll help you move your stuff."

CHAPTER 12

Lia lay propped up on the pillows of their bed while she waited for her men.

Their bed.

Her men.

Holy hell. Only a month ago she would've never believed this was possible.

But it was. And the last two weeks had been amazing. They'd developed their own routine, and she'd gotten to know their habits and quirks.

Like, for instance, that Travis loved it when she played with his balls while she sucked his dick, and Cam was a sucker for a little assplay of his own.

Speaking of assplay ... that was exactly what she was waiting for. Because they'd been holding out on her. And that was going to stop tonight.

The door creaked open, and excitement bloomed inside her.

"Baby, you in here?" Travis yelled from the door.

"Mmmmhmmm ... and I'm waiting for you," Lia called back.

Footsteps sounded as he closed in on the bedroom. Travis's head swiveled in a double take—probably because she was naked and laid out on the bed. "Hell, you have no idea how much I want to just climb in with you, but I can't. Ro's in labor. Baby's on the way."

"Oh, shit." Lia pushed to her knees and scooted off the bed. She ran to grab a T-shirt and jeans. "What can I do? Is she okay?"

"I think she's fine, but we're all on high alert. Her dad's pacing, her sister's pacing, and Graham and Zach are pacing. It's like this whole place is holding its breath."

"Where's Cam?"

"He just swapped out with Graham's watch. Ro and Allison have known that the baby was coming for a few hours, but she didn't want to get G and Zach fired up until it was a little closer in time. So now shit's moving along real quick. I'm going to relieve Ryan because Zach was up next to cover him."

"Okay. Well, I guess I'll go ... help? Pace? I don't even know."

"I think Ty is in the kitchen pulling together some food since Allison is with Rowan."

"Yes. Food. I can do that."

Travis held out his hand. "I'll walk you over there."

Lia smoothed her hair back into a ponytail and grabbed an elastic off the dresser to secure it. She crossed the room to where Travis stood and took his hand.

Looking up into his gorgeous face, she said, "You know you don't need to walk me everywhere anymore, right? I'm ... I'm good. I'm not going to freak."

Travis reached up and stroked along her cheekbone with his thumb. "I know you're good. I've been watching you come into your own for months, and the last couple weeks have just been the icing on the cake. You've always been stronger than you realize, Lia. I'm just glad you're figuring that out."

A rush of warmth fluttered through her. The conviction with which he said the words, the softness with which he touched her. They were just two of the many things she loved about him.

"Thank you." They were the only words that came to mind. "Thank you for believing in me."

He lifted her hand to his lips and pressed the sweetest kiss to her knuckles. "Thank you for letting me be part of this with you and Cam. I know if you'd had to choose, you would've—"

Lia raised her finger and pressed it to her lips. "Don't even say it. It's the three of us against the world. Always. No matter what."

His smile unfurled and lifted her heart. "Come on. Let's get going."

Travis had mixed feelings about manning the watch post at the front gate. It was the most interesting of the posts because of the location, but the action he saw up there usually broke his heart. Discouraging people from thinking about coming inside the fence line was tough. Usually the business end of an M-16 did the job, but there'd been a couple occasions where they'd had to show how serious they were about protecting their own. Thank God they'd never been faced with turning women or children away, because Travis wasn't sure he'd be able to do it.

With remains of the government and the military rising again in the last few months, and the rumors of the New Hope for America Work Corps camps trickling in through a few of their outside radio contacts, things were more dangerous than ever. Which was why the man approaching the fence line, hands in the air, rubbed Travis the wrong fucking way. He was wearing a uniform. Given the state of the military, that uniform might mean nothing—could be a left over from the Corps or a deserter from the new regime.

The man came closer, and Travis rested his finger alongside the trigger and sighted him in, positioning the guy's head in the crosshairs of his riflescope. His trigger finger froze when he recognized the guy's face.

With his other hand, he reached for the radio. "Command, I got an update on the uniform at the gate ... I think I know him from our last tour in the Sandbox. He was a Gunny. Fuck, can't remember his name though. Just remember the way he yelled."

Jonah, Allison's husband, replied, "No shit? I've gotta let G know. He's gonna want to hear this."

"Dude, he's got a kid coming."

Jonah replied, "From the way the screaming has quieted down to nothing, I'm thinking the kid's here. He'll fucking have my balls if I don't tell him."

"Fine, do what you gotta do. I'm going to get a closer look."

"Your timing sucks ass, Richardson," Graham said, as he met Travis and Jackson Richardson just inside the front gate.

"You know how fucking long I've been on the road to get here? I'm lucky I even fucking made it. They're shooting deserters on sight these days," Jackson growled.

"Still can't believe you did it," Travis said.

At Jackson's sharp look, he raised a hand. "I'm not judging. I would've done the same thing. We've been hearing awful shit. Soldiers killing civilians who don't go quietly into the camps. No fucking way I'd do it. Women and children? That shit ain't right."

"It's way worse than you've heard, man. So much fucking worse. But that ain't why I'm here. I'm here because I figured if anyone had news around here, it'd be you guys."

"What kind of news you looking for?"

"I'm looking for a girl."

"A girl?" Graham asked. "You lose someone?"

He nodded. "Yeah. It's a long fucking story, but the gist of it is, she was snatched by some redneck fuckers about five miles away from here a few days after the shit hit the fan. I got shot, almost died. Would've died if the guy who'd found me hadn't seen my dog tags and hauled my ass to the nearest military camp and handed me over. Took me all this time to recover and make my way back here. I've got nothing to go on, and no one in town has any clue what happened to her."

Travis's stomach churned at the story. He'd been shot. Five miles from here. The girl had been snatched by some redneck fuckers. Jesus.

"What's her name?" Travis asked.

Jackson's eyes shot to his, and the pain in them was real and vivid.

"Lia."

CHAPTER 13

Lia hummed as she set dinner on the table in the mess hall. The men were filing in. She was finally contributing to their little community—and it was gratifying.

The screen door cracked open, and Lia looked up. A smile stretched across her face instinctively at the sight of Travis, but faded when she couldn't read whatever was reflected on his face.

"What's wrong? Are Ro and the baby okay?" she asked.

"They're fine. Little girl's name is Mira. She's healthy and beautiful."

"Then what—?" Her words broke off when she saw the man standing behind him. Her legs turned to Jell-O, and she sank to her knees. "Oh my God," she breathed.

"Lia, honey. Holy shit, you're alive."

"Jack. Omigod. Omigod."

She pushed off the floor and stumbled to her feet.

They met in the center of the room, and he lifted her up and swung her around.

"Cannot believe you're here. I've been looking for you, girl."

"I thought you were dead. I thought..." Tears burst free and streamed down her cheeks.

For long moments, Cam stood beside Travis and watched as Lia bawled in her brother's arms. He was happy as fuck the man wasn't dead, but he wanted to dry her tears and make sure she never cried again. Screw the happy tears bullshit—no tears from Lia were good tears, in his opinion.

When Lia's brother finally lowered her to the ground, she immediately threw herself at Travis. Cam didn't even think, he stepped up and closed the circle around her, and they both held her while she laughed and cried some more.

The hard "What the fuck, man?" from Jackson had him lifting his head.

Lia turned in their arms and faced her brother. She tensed, and Cam knew it was because of the disapproval clearly branded on her brother's features. Cam dropped his eyes to Lia's face, and all of the joy that had been there was fading away.

Cam manned up. "She's ours, man. I know it's a little different arrangement from what you're probably used to ... but—"

Jack's expression darkened. "What the fuck are you talking about? Lia, get over here."

"I know she's your sister, but even you don't get to talk to her like that," Travis bit out.

"Lia," Jack growled again.

"Enough," Lia said. "All of you." She turned to Cam. "I think I need to have a word with my brother. In private."

As much as he didn't want to let her go, he knew he didn't have a choice.

"We'll be right here waiting when you're done, sweetheart." He didn't bother to look at Jack as he pressed a kiss to her temple. A disapproving brother wasn't going to change a damn thing between them. He wouldn't let it.

He's alive. The words chanted in Lia's head on repeat as she led Jack toward the cabin she used to share with Erica. She wasn't sure why she went there, but she did. Maybe because she didn't want her brother in the space she shared with Cam and Travis.

She pushed open the door and was thankful to find it empty. She took a seat on her old twin bed and nodded to Erica's. "Feel free to have a seat."

There was a table and two chairs in one corner of the cabin, but they were covered in Erica's clothes and other stuff.

They sat knee to knee, and Jack grabbed her hand and held it between his. "I didn't come here to fight with you. Fuck, I'm not going to fight with you. I've spent the last nine months going crazy not knowing where you were and how you were doing. Or fuck, if you were even..." he trailed off, but Lia finished for him.

"If I was alive? I know the feeling. The last glimpse I got of you was you in a pool of blood. I thought you were dead. I didn't think anyone could live through that ... not without regularly functioning hospitals and surgeons."

Jack squeezed her hand. "I almost died. More than once. Hell. Infections, dehydration—you name it, it almost killed me. But I'm a stubborn son of a bitch, and I wasn't going to let anything take me out. And I never lost hope of finding you. Saving you."

She squeezed his hand back. "I don't need saving anymore. I've got real heroes right here. Without them ... I would've died. Either the men who kidnapped me would've done it, or I would've finished the job for them."

Jack's eyes slammed closed, and his features creased. "I'm so sorry I couldn't protect you. I should've—"

"You didn't even have a gun. There was nothing you could do."

He dropped her hand and jammed his fingers into his thick, dark hair. "I'm a fucking Marine, shit was going down. I shouldn't have stepped away from the house without a gun. I was just in such a fucking hurry that day. I didn't even fucking think." He shook his head. "I'll never forgive myself for that."

"There's nothing to forgive." Lia swallowed, unable to believe she was about to say what was on the tip of her tongue. But it was the truth. "Besides, if things hadn't happened the way they did, I would've never met Cam and Travis, and that..."

Jack looked up at her. "Lia, I know this world is crazy, but two—"

"I'm in love with them. *Both* of them. And yes, this world is crazy, and maybe that craziness gave me the courage to follow my heart, but I wouldn't change a thing. You don't understand how happy they make me. How *safe* they make me feel." She reached back out and grabbed his hand. "I never thought I'd feel safe again after what happened to me, but ... I do. And it's because of them. Instead of growling about the oddity of our relationship, you should be thanking them."

Jack's brown eyes—so much like her own—met hers. "I know. But I'm still your big brother, and today has been a hell of a shock for both of us. I just ... need some time to get used to the idea, okay?"

"Speaking of time, do you have plans? How long can you stay?" Lia started to panic. "I don't want to lose you when I just found you again. That would be too much to handle. I can't—"

"Hey, hey. No reason to get excited about it. I'll talk to the guys and see if they can put me to work in exchange for letting me stay. I don't want to be a drain on resources. I've got skills to offer up."

Lia hadn't even thought of that. "They'll let you stay, I know they will. I won't let them make you leave." She didn't have any pull, but Cam and Travis did, and she wasn't above begging. In creative ways.

"We've got a lot to catch up on. You want to go first, or do you want me to?" The question was the last one Lia really wanted to answer, but this was her brother. She could tell him most of it. Okay, maybe not most, but a little. Very little, when it came to Cam and Travis.

"How about you go first?"

He nodded. "Well, I woke up not knowing where the fuck I was..."

CHAPTER 14

Cam sat stiffly in his chair in the mess hall, waiting for Lia to come back. A glance at Travis revealed his similar posture. They'd both pushed around the venison chili and cornbread that Lia had made.

Fuck, Jack Richardson's little sister. He hardly knew the guy, but he'd respected what little he'd known. A good Marine. Solid leader. Liked and respected by his own men. And now he was probably trying to talk Lia into leaving with him.

Won't fucking happen. He wasn't letting her go.

But what if she wants to go? A voice in his head taunted. *You can't make her stay.*

But she wouldn't want to leave, would she? And fuck, even beyond the fact that losing her would shred his heart, the safest place for her was inside the walls of this compound. That just meant one thing: they had to talk Jack into staying. There was no other choice.

Being an only child of parents who'd died within months of each other when he was in his early twenties, Cam could only imagine what it'd be like to think he'd lost a sibling and then gotten him back. He wouldn't want to let him out of his sight.

That meant they'd also have to get Jack on board with the relationship they had. His approval mattered, because it would be important to Lia.

"What the fuck are we going to do if he tries to get her to leave with him?" Travis asked.

"Ain't happening." Cam laid out his plan, and Travis nodded.

"Agreed. Him staying is a good idea. I mean, another mouth to feed, but he's built like us, would protect this place to the death with Lia inside, and if the new military comes knocking on our door, not only does he know how they operate, but he's not going to hesitate to choose sides. You want to talk to Graham, or want me to?"

Since Graham was the leader of the crew and had been the catalyst behind the ranch and compound, his approval was necessary.

"I'll talk to G. No problem."

"And how do we handle the protective big brother angle?" Travis asked.

"We let Lia take the lead. He's her family. We back her up however she needs."

"Sounds good."

As soon as the words had come out of Travis's mouth, the door to the mess hall opened, and Lia and Jack stepped inside.

Lia walked directly to them, a smile on her face. She stopped in front of Cam, and he hesitated. He wanted to pull her into his lap, but her brother watched, not looking like he wanted to ram his fist through any vital organs. Cam wasn't sure he wanted to change that particular attitude by crossing what big brother might consider a line. At least not right now. If Jack stayed, he was going to have to get used to it.

Instead, Cam caught one of Lia's hands and brought her palm to his mouth and kissed it. "Everything good?"

She nodded. "Everything's really good. Or ... it will be when you tell me that Jack will be able to stay."

The concern that had been plaguing Cam dissipated. "He wants to stay?"

"Yes. Now that he's officially a ... deserter, it's not safe for him out there either. And I can't lose him again."

She blinked, and Cam's gut twisted at the thought of her crying again. "Don't worry, sweetheart. If Jack wants to stay, I'll make sure G lets him stay. We were thinking the same damn thing. Family's too important—and scarce—to let it walk away these days."

"Good," Lia whispered. "I was hoping you'd say that."

Travis stood. "Graham's busy with Ro and Zach and the baby, but I'll see about finding Jack a place to stay."

"Beau's got an empty bedroom in his cabin," Cam offered. He looked to Jack. "It's a king bed or the bunkroom and a single."

Jack smiled broadly. "I'm no fool. I'll take the king if he's cool with a roommate."

"Good deal." Cam stood and held out his hand. "It's good to see you again, Richardson." A thought struck him, and he looked from Lia to Jack. "Why don't you have the same last name?"

"Half-siblings. My mom didn't change my name after she remarried. She wanted me to have a piece of my dad, I think. He passed away when I was two."

"Sorry, man."

Jack shrugged. "Just makes it more and more clear why family is so important."

"That's the truth. I'll go check with Beau and see about getting you set up. Lia, sweetheart, want to get your brother some of that venison chili? You kicked ass with that."

Jack's eyebrows went up. "She cooks now too? Damn, things really have changed."

Cam smiled and headed for the door, a smile tugging at his lips, because shit was going to work out just fine.

CHAPTER 15

Saying goodnight to her brother and then walking back to the cabin she shared with Cam and Travis was a touch surreal, and Lia didn't question the happiness that thrummed through her.

"I still can't believe he's *alive*, and that he's *here*," she said. "It's ... amazing."

Cam's arm tightened around her shoulders, and Travis's hand gripped hers tighter.

"Believe it, babe," Travis said.

"I feel like ... everything is exactly the way it should be."

"It is," Cam replied. "And if there's anything you want to change, you just let us know."

Travis held open the door, and Lia stepped inside. Her earlier thoughts and plans resurfaced as soon as the bed came into view.

She was done waiting.

Turning, she pressed a hand to each of their chests as they entered the bedroom. They both followed her as she circled them and pushed them backward to the bed. When the mattress hit the backs of their legs, she shoved, and they both sat.

"There is one thing."

She reached for the hem of her shirt, tugged it up over her head, and tossed it on the floor at their feet.

"Whatever the one thing is, consider me on board," Travis replied, hunger edging his tone. Lia met his eyes to see the same hunger reflected there.

"Good." She shifted her gaze to Cam as she reached for the button of her jeans. "You feel the same way?"

"Anything that keeps you stripping works for me."

A rush of feminine power filled Lia.

She flicked the button open and slid the zipper down before shimmying her hips and kicking off her jeans.

She'd taken to going commando on a regular basis, and both men groaned when she rid herself of that last piece of clothing.

"Come here, sweetheart," Cam ordered.

"Only if you promise to give me what I want."

Brows furrowed, Travis asked, "What?"

"I think you know."

Lia thought of the ways they'd taken her, and the one way they *hadn't*.

She strutted forward, confident in her movements, and sat on the bed between them. Her words were just as bold as her movements. "I want you in my ass."

Her words hung in the air as she pushed herself back on the bed. Cam and Travis turned in unison to stare at her.

Cam crawled up onto his knees beside her, his hand skimming from her ankle to her breast. His rough palm cupped her as he lowered his lips to her ear.

"You sure you're ready for this, sweetheart? Me in your ass and Trav in your pussy? Filling you fuller than you've ever been? Are you ready for how hard we're going to make you come?"

She was sure he could feel her whole body tremble and vibrate along his lips.

"Yes," she breathed.

"Good girl," he said before closing his teeth over her earlobe. The move ignited more shivers. Another hand landed on her thigh and parted her legs.

Pulling her eyes from Cam, she saw Travis lowering his face to her pussy. He spread her open with two fingers before his lips and tongue made contact.

Good Lord, she loved their foreplay.

Lia knew she'd be begging within minutes. Begging for what only the two of them could give her. Cam slid his lips down to her right nipple and added to the sensations already gathering low and tight in her belly.

"More. Please. More." She didn't care that she was begging.

Travis lifted his head. "She's ready, man. So fucking ready."

Cam nodded and reached for the nightstand drawer.

He pulled out a bottle of lube and tossed a condom to Travis. He tore another open with his teeth and rolled it on.

Travis lay on the bed, flat on his back beside her. He pressed a kiss to her lips—a kiss where she tasted herself on his tongue—and told her, "On your knees, baby. I want my cock inside that sweet pussy before Cam takes your ass."

She didn't hesitate to follow orders. Lia had waited what seemed like forever for this final step. She sat up, threw her leg over his waist, and gripped his cock. Positioning him at her entrance, she sank down, moaning as he filled every inch.

He was so big that Lia wondered for the hundredth time how her body would accommodate them both, but she had to believe it was possible.

"This ass is so fucking perfect. I've been dying to get inside you." Cam's fingers trailed along her spine until one rested over the pucker of her ass. A cool drizzle of what she assumed was the lube followed, and Cam began to play.

The added sensation from Cam made her want to buck against Travis and ride him until they both came, but a light slap landed on her ass.

"Stay still, sweetheart. We're going to take this slow."

The pressure on her ass increased until Cam pushed one finger inside her. Then another. He pumped them in and out and she reveled in the slight burn and edge of pleasure-pain that accompanied it. More lube and slow, steady movements had her hips rocking. Travis lifted a hand to skim along her hip and press a thumb down over her clit.

"Oh God. I'm going to come if you keep doing that," she breathed.

"That's kind of the point," he replied.

Finally, the pressure on her ass faded away, until she felt the blunt head of Cam's cock press against it.

"Breathe, baby. Don't forget to breathe," Travis ordered.

Lia breathed, and the hand on her lower back pressed her down toward Travis's chest.

Pressure. A twinge of pain. And then...

"Omigod. You're ... Omigod."

Shivers were no longer shivers. They were electrically charged bolts of lightning ripping through her body. Her nipples hardened, and every nerve ending in her body tightened to the breaking point.

Lia had never felt so fully *possessed* in her life.

"You good, sweetheart?" Cam asked, his hand stroking her back and side. "You ready for us to move?"

She nodded. Words were almost beyond her reach, but she managed a shaky, "Please."

"Good girl."

Travis gripped her hips as Cam pulled back, lifting her up and off his cock as Cam slid back inside.

In-out-in-out. The rhythm of the two men, taking her together, emptied every thought from her head except mindless pleasure.

"Touch yourself, sweetheart," Cam ordered. "Play with that sweet little clit. I want you to fall apart when you come. We'll be here to pick up the pieces."

Lia obeyed, because ... just because.

Her fingers found her clit, and she pressed and teased and circled as the men dragged her to the brink.

Over and over they took turns filling her, fucking her. Until every single thread of her control pulled tight— and snapped.

Lia screamed as an orgasm unlike any other tore through her.

Falling forward onto Travis, she clutched at his shoulders, burying her face in his neck. Her teeth dug into the muscle of his shoulder as she splintered into smaller and smaller pieces. She was barely conscious of the two groans that came within moments.

Limp, sated, and completely destroyed, Lia closed her eyes and passed out.

Travis curled around Lia as her head rested on Cam's chest. She'd been totally out after they'd finished, only waking as they'd cleaned her up and tucked her in.

She'd mumbled 'I love yous' and promptly passed out again.

It wasn't hard on their egos; that was for damn sure.

He let his mind wander to what was next.

A new life had been born on Castle Creek land today. A new era was beginning.

Life before the grid went down was fading to a distant memory as they all adapted to this new reality.

The future was uncertain, and nothing was guaranteed but the fact that they'd do whatever it took to keep this ranch and the people on it safe.

The family was growing, and he wondered if he and Cam and Lia would add to it themselves one of these days. The thought of bringing a child into this crazy, dangerous world was terrifying, but the idea of Lia growing round with their baby filled him with a sense of possessive rightness.

They'd let fate take its course.

Closing his eyes, he slid into sleep. The last thought in his head before he drifted off was: *I wouldn't change a goddamn thing.*

EPILOGUE

"It's my turn to hold the baby," Erica declared.

"Oh, hell no. You had Mira for at least a half hour earlier. It's totally my turn," Lia said. Her eyes rested on the infant sleeping in Ro's arms.

"I never realized I'd have to fight to hold my own kid," Ro replied, settling Mira in Lia's arms.

"It's not our fault you make such adorable ones," Erica remarked, her voice quieting as she sat beside Lia and trailed a finger down the little girl's soft cheek. "There's so much Graham in her. I guess you'll have to let Zach's swimmers win next time."

Ro raised her eyebrows. "One at a time. I'm not thinking about anything beyond Mira for now." Ro looked to Lia. "What about you? I see the way those two watch you when you have her." Lia's eyes landed on the men coming in the door of the mess hall, and warmth settled over her at the idea.

Blessed didn't even begin to cover how she felt.

Cam's eyes were soft as he stopped next to her and sank into a crouch.

"You look beautiful holding her. But then again, you always look beautiful," he whispered.

"Thank you. And she's the beautiful one."

Jack stopped behind Cam. "Always figured you'd have a whole brood of your own, all the babysitting you did as a kid."

Lia smiled at Cam and Travis. "I guess we'll see what happens. Here you go, Daddy." She handed Mira off to Zach as he came close with that look in his eyes. The one that said he needed to hold his daughter.

The thought of Cam or Travis coming to her with that look made her want to tell them to skip the condoms forever.

Lia stood, and each man held out a hand. She gripped them both and let them lead her out of the mess hall toward their cabin.

Lifting her face to the sky, she soaked up the light and said goodbye to the darkness forever.

NEVER MISS AN UPDATE!

OTHER TITLES BY MEGHAN MARCH

Beneath this Mask
Beneath this Ink
Beneath these Chains

CONNECT WITH MEGHAN MARCH

Website: www.meghanmarch.com
Facebook: www.facebook.com/MeghanMarchAuthor
Twitter: www.twitter.com/Meghan_March
Instagram: www.instagram.com/MeghanMarch
Pinterest: www.pinterest.com/MeghanMarch1
Tsu: www.tsu.co/MeghanMarch
Goodreads: www.goodreads.com/MeghanMarchAuthor

UNAPOLOGETICALLY SEXY ROMANCE

Made in the USA
Middletown, DE
03 January 2017